escaping indigo
BOOK ONE

escaping
indigo

✕

ELI LANG

RIPTIDE
PUBLISHING

Riptide Publishing
PO Box 1537
Burnsville, NC 28714
www.riptidepublishing.com

Escaping Indigo

Cover art: Natasha Snow, natashasnowdesigns.com
Editors: Sarah Lyons, May Peterson, maypetersonbooks.com
Layout: L.C. Chase, lcchase.com/design.htm

ISBN: 978-1-62649-591-3

First edition
July, 2017

Also available in ebook:
ISBN: 978-1-62649-590-6

escaping indigo
BOOK ONE

escaping indigo

ELI LANG

RIPTIDE
PUBLISHING

For Small Black, who rescued me when I was feeling low.
And to AC for being the only person I want in my band.

TABLE OF
contents

chapter one

X

i wondered, sometimes, when exactly it was you could tell yourself you'd made it. When you could let yourself believe it. After your first show? After the first big venue? The first album? The first song to chart past one hundred? Past ten? Or was it when another band, a band you knew and loved, recognized you, called you by your first name, clapped you on the shoulder and said they loved your new songs? Was there ever a moment that you could look back on as the defining one?

I didn't know the answer, because I'd never gotten there. Never reached a point where I could pause and look around, and tell myself that I'd really managed something. Really done something important. That we'd made it. Every new thing had been the most success I'd ever had, in a band, as a musician. But there had never been a time when I'd told myself that this was *it*. That I'd done what I'd set out to do and everything else after *this moment* was extra.

It was funny, because all that time—when we'd been writing music and gigging, all the times we'd been auditioning yet another bass player or keyboardist, when we'd been scrambling for every cent so we could drive to another city for a show, so we could put our album out, so we could make sure we had merch—I'd never felt anything even close to what I imagined that particular, pivotal moment felt like. That arrival. It had all been a frantic rush instead, no time to really think at all. Only time to swim as hard as we could and hope our heads stayed above water.

But I wasn't in my own band anymore. Now I was in a gaudy but still rock-appropriate-grungy Chicago theater, working for someone else, for a band that wasn't mine. Standing on the side of the wide stage instead of at the front of it. Handing out guitars and setting up drums instead of playing my own drums. Helping someone else entertain a crowd instead of doing it with my own band. And it should have been depressing as fuck. It should have been the worst place I could possibly have ended up. But it wasn't. And when the band's singer Bellamy turned away from the microphone and caught my eye, threw me that cocky half smile like he sometimes did, even though I knew he did that for a hundred people in the audience every night, it was almost like I'd made it, instead of having fallen.

That night, I watched from my spot off stage while Escaping Indigo, the band I now worked for, played. They seemed almost better than usual, pushing the music into all the corners of the room, out into the parking lot. The first few shows of the tour had gone well, and they were riding that energy. Bellamy jumped down from the stage to stand with the audience. People reached out to touch him while he sang, pulled at him until he had to hold the mic up and tilt his chin back to get the words out. A hand slithered up the front of his shirt, and he tugged it out, but then he held on to it, twisting his fingers with the other person's. Everybody wanted a piece of him, something that they could make their own, and he made it seem like they could have that. I knew that feeling. I'd been a fan, the biggest fan, long before I'd ever imagined I'd end up being their roadie.

After, with the sounds of the show still ringing in my head, when the silence around me was almost smothering and my ears felt as if they'd been stuffed with cotton, I went around to the side of the building. It was darker and quieter there. I wanted to have one more cigarette before I headed to the bus and to bed. Instead, I ran into Bellamy. I wasn't sure it was him at first—I had a moment when I panicked and figured I was about to get murdered in a city I'd never even set foot in before today, but then I saw the black jacket, the skinny jeans, the slight wave in the coppery-brown hair, and I recognized him.

"Got a light?"

His voice was soft, just this side of hoarse. I could still hear him, like an echo in my mind, calling out to the audience, singing songs I knew all the words to, his voice strong and sure, velvety. It was rougher now, but I could hear that richness behind his words, the depth he could coax out of it.

I dug around in my pocket, fumbling for my lighter. He took a step back, into the shadows, and I followed. When I flicked the lighter, the flame lit up his face, highlighted the angles of his cheekbones, made the makeup around his eyes stand out, stark and black against his skin. He held his cigarette up for me, breathed in, then moved away. I took out my own pack and lit one for myself.

Bellamy leaned against the wall. He wiggled his shoulders a little, settling in, getting as comfortable as he could. He drew on his cigarette once, but then he pulled it away and held it by his hip, tucked between two fingers.

I didn't know whether I should stay or go. Bellamy and I had been traveling together, obviously, and we'd spoken, but never much more than "Good morning," and "Good show," and "Please tune this guitar like this." He'd been kind and polite, but standoffish. And I . . . I had been so nervous to meet him, to be around him, that I'd basically clammed up every time he was near me. It'd be nice to be able to actually have a conversation with him, but I didn't want to intrude on his solitude. And I didn't know what conversation I'd be able to come up with, anyway.

I took a tiny step back, and my foot scraped against a patch of gravel. Bellamy jerked his head up and glanced over at me.

I was probably blushing already. I blushed hard and obviously, despite how tan I was, and it was probably visible, even in the dim light here. I waved my hand over my shoulder, trying to play it cool.

"I'll, ah . . ."

His hand snapped out and grabbed my wrist, but not hard. Only enough to keep me here, enough for me to feel his touch on my skin. Then he let go. "You don't need to go." He turned away again, but I didn't think he was blocking me out. He tilted his head against the building and stared up at the sky. It was clear, but the city lights were too bright, even back here, and there weren't any stars to see. "I was . . . looking for a place to come down, you know?"

I stepped forward this time, and leaned against the wall next to him. Not close enough to touch, but enough that I could feel the warmth of him, smell the smoke of his cigarette, earthy and bitter. I took a drag off my own, but it seemed almost beside the point, now.

"I missed this," he said, soft, his voice fading away, blending into the sounds of traffic and people shouting and laughing.

I turned my head to him. His profile was all in shadow, just a sharp nose and chin, hair that was a bit too long. He looked as much like a rock star standing still as he did when he was moving around on stage. He gave off an energy, more contained now, but no less forceful in its magnetism. I thought of him like a live wire, something dangerous and electric and lovely.

"I missed being on the road." He glanced at me. "There isn't anything as good as touring, as playing."

I nodded. That made sense. I supposed it was different for everyone—I knew some people liked the recording the best, and thought the touring was a chore—but there was definitely something raw and beautiful about this, even when it was tedious or uncomfortable.

"I'm glad you have the bus, though," I blurted out. "Quinn said you used to ride around in a van."

Bellamy laughed, loudly. "We did. Not for a few tours now. But, god, that was a pain in the ass. We were all so crammed together. This is better. But it was fun." He trailed off, and he sounded almost wistful. I could imagine it. There was something freeing about being on tour, no matter how you got there. Quinn had told me about the van like it was his own personal hell, though. He'd laid a nearly reverent hand on the bus, and the expression I'd seen on his face had made me laugh out loud. It had reminded me of how long he'd been working with the band, from the time they'd been tiny and he'd been the only roadie they'd had, to where they were now, just big enough to have a tour bus, big enough that we had somewhere comfortable to sleep instead of shitty hotel rooms.

"Are you liking it?" Bellamy asked, surprising me out of my thoughts. "Being on the road?"

I took in a deep breath, but I tried not to make it sound like that was what I was doing. I thought about the first time I'd been able to say I was on tour, when I'd been a drummer and not a roadie. When it had been *my* band out on the road. It was laughable, because we'd only stopped in three cities before we'd gone home, and it hadn't been anything like this. No tour bus, no roadies, no venues that held hundreds of people. We'd driven a friend's van, like Escaping Indigo had once, packed with our stuff, and we'd slept in the back on a tiny pile of blankets. We'd carried our own gear, set up by ourselves. And we sure as shit hadn't been headlining. But the crowds had liked us all right. We'd sold some of the handmade CDs we'd brought, with our initials written on them in place of a band name, because we never could decide, and people had asked us if we were going to be coming by again. It hadn't been like this at all. But it had been good. It had felt *so good*. Freeing and exciting and like we'd been on the brink of something incredible.

"I like it," I said. I thought about adding something else to it, to explain that I'd done this before, but not in the same way. To keep the conversation going, more than anything. But I didn't want to bring all of that here, into this quiet space between us, and I didn't know Bellamy well enough to guess how he'd react.

He didn't ask me for any more than that, though. He slid me a wry smile. "But you were hoping for a quiet place too, huh? And now I'm talking your ear off."

I smiled back. "I don't mind." Bellamy could talk to me anytime. I'd never even imagined I'd be able to stand here with him, like this. He'd been an untouchable idol for so long that this felt unreal.

He dropped his cigarette and ground it out, then bent and scooped it up into his hand. "It's good to have a quiet space." He turned to me. "Touring's the best, but it'll wear you down, being with everyone all the time."

"And I intruded into your space, this time," I answered, asking without words whether that was okay.

He shrugged. "I didn't mind, either. My boyfriend and I used to sneak away. Find the dark corners. He was a roadie for us too. So it's . . ." he laughed, "similar." His smile went lopsided and sad. "But not the same. Sorry, that was awkward."

I shook my head. "Why isn't he working this tour?"

"'Cause he dumped me," Bellamy answered without skipping a beat. "Middle of last tour, he up and left, no note, no nothing. Guess he'd had enough."

"Oh."

"Yeah." He took a step, and I couldn't see his face anymore in the dark. "Hey, I'm glad you came over. I was worried about . . . It was good to talk to someone. Thanks."

I nodded. I didn't know what else to say, but it didn't matter. He nodded back and then headed off, in the direction of the bus. I stood outside for a little longer, took the last drag on my cigarette. I thought about Bellamy picking his up, careful not to litter, about the way the fine lines around his eyes had tightened when he'd talked about his ex. He'd told me about it like it was simply a thing that had happened, but I wondered if that was what he really felt about it.

I wondered, too, who would be stupid enough to dump someone as talented and gorgeous as Bellamy.

X

I didn't exactly try to avoid Bellamy over the next day, as we drove, but I didn't seek him out, either. I was still mulling over our short conversation. I'd only ever really thought of Bellamy as a rock star, even for the short time I'd been his roadie. And he definitely was a rock star in my eyes, even if his band hadn't yet reached, might never reach, the level where they played stadium shows and slept in luxury hotel rooms. That was nice as far as status went, but I was interested in the *music*, and Bellamy made music like no one else could. He shone, so bright, whether I was watching him play a show, or listening to his voice through my headphones. I'd never thought of him in any other way. But the night before, as much as he'd still sparkled, he'd seemed . . . more contained. A person instead of a figure. Quiet and focused inward.

It was easy enough not to bump into him. We had the whole tour bus to spread out on—two rooms, a large front one and a cozier back room, where one or two of us would sometimes go for some privacy, plus the middle section where our bunks were. And even though it had only been a few days, we'd sorted out spots for ourselves, and we tended to stick with them. Sometimes Bellamy wrote music with Tuck or played a video game with Ava, but more often than not, he tucked himself into a corner of a couch with a book or his guitar, or had a quiet conversation with Lissa, our merch person and Tuck's girlfriend.

We all tended to congregate in the front room, but even then, my spot was at the end of the room, opposite Bellamy's, so we were still apart, just enough to make conversation difficult.

We parked for the evening in Columbus, Ohio, at the next venue. In the dead time between sound check and the show itself, I walked around the building, to the back parking lot, hoping to sneak in a cigarette and some time to myself, and walked almost smack into Bellamy. Again. It was like déjà vu of the night before, except it was light out now, and I almost laughed at the ridiculousness of it.

Bellamy must have heard me come up beside him, same as last time, but this time, instead of asking me for a light, he waved me over. He was sitting with his back against the building's side wall. Most of the sidewalk he was sitting on was in the shade, but he had his feet stuck out into a patch of sunlight. I walked over, but stopped before sitting down.

"Aren't you getting some quiet time again?" I asked.

A smile flickered over his mouth. "Awful lot of space one musician needs, huh?"

I shook my head. "I can see this being stressful." Hell, I knew it was. I just didn't know it like he did.

He shrugged. "Come sit. Don't stand there hovering over me."

I lowered myself down next to him, but instead of continuing a conversation with me, he turned to face forward again. He was staring off across the street. There was a tiny neighborhood there, small scraps of lawn passing as backyards. He watched the grass move with the breeze and seemed very much like he didn't have a single care in the world. I couldn't help staring at him, taken by him in this moment of almost stillness. He was smoking again, as slow as last time, his hand moving in a lazy arc from where it rested on his knee to his mouth and back. The wind was tossing his bangs in his face. His skin looked almost translucent, his cheeks flushed pink with the late-summer heat, and his body was as relaxed and elegant as it was on stage. He came across so comfortable, so confident, even though there was no one to see him, no one he had to impress. It was natural for him.

I wanted to sit for a minute, and take in the smell of the soil and the breeze on my skin and Bellamy beside me. It was quiet out here, a quiet you didn't get while stuck on a tour bus, or when you were always in a new city, a new venue filled with people, taking and giving instructions, with music and banter such a constant background noise that it became a hum that it felt strange to be without. The wind through the dry grass and the distant sound of traffic were the only noises here, and I thought if I listened hard enough, I could hear the soft scrape of Bellamy's finger against his cigarette, the shift of his T-shirt against his skin. His breath, moving in and out of him, slow and steady.

"What were you going to say, last night?" I asked without thinking.

He turned toward me, slow, like he was coming back from somewhere else. "What?"

There was that blush again, hot and probably so much more visible here in the daylight. "Never mind."

His hair tangled in his eyes, and he reached up and pushed it aside with two fingers, his cigarette still tucked firmly between the others. Then he glanced away, took one last drag of his cigarette, and stubbed it out on the ground next to him. His movements were efficient, but unhurried. "No, what?"

I clasped my hands together. I hadn't gotten out my own cigarettes, and I wished I had, just to have something to do. I twisted my fingers together instead. "Last night, you said you were worried about something. But then you didn't say what. And I . . . wondered."

"Oh." He stared down at his knees, the sun creeping up his jeans. "Sorry. I wasn't trying to be coy. I was just tired."

I nodded and stared across the street. I wanted to kick myself for asking at all. It was as good as prying. But I was . . . curious. Had been curious about it since he'd let it slip. Had been curious about him long before that.

"I was worried about being on tour," he said after a minute, when I'd been sure he wouldn't say anything at all. "I love it so much, but I . . ." He trailed off, and I held my hand up.

"You don't have to tell me. I shouldn't have asked." I couldn't even make myself quite meet his eyes. I was mortified.

His hand brushed my shoulder, so soft I wasn't sure it had actually happened. But when I looked over, he was watching me. "My boyfriend leaving . . . It messed me up. I wasn't . . ." He took a deep breath. "I wasn't myself. I was in a bad place, and it's taken me a long time to get away from that. And I was worried that being on tour again might . . . put me there again."

"I get that." I could have told him, then, exactly how much I understood it, but I couldn't quite make myself do it. This was his conversation, and I wasn't going to hijack it with my own story.

"Yeah?"

I nodded. "Has it? Brought you back there?"

He slumped against the wall. "Here and there. Little things. I'm still . . ." He waved his hand through the air, and I wanted to ask, because I was only more curious now, not less. But I couldn't do that, either. He shifted to face me, and his lips lifted at one side in a smile that was wry and unhappy. "Sometimes I get . . . nervous. Stressed. That's all. I'll be fine, I think."

I nodded again. I didn't know what else to do. We sat there together for a while longer, and it wasn't as uncomfortable as I'd have imagined. It wasn't, actually, uncomfortable at all. We watched the trickle of traffic move past, watched people go about their day, and I soaked up the sights of a city I'd never set foot in before this. The sights I was willing to bet most tourists never saw at all. I liked seeing places from this view, from the back alleys and parking lots, from street level.

I had to get up after a while, so I could go help Quinn. He probably wouldn't need me quite yet, but I figured I'd intruded on Bellamy's space enough already. He stopped me when I turned to go, though, like he had the night before. He said my name this time instead of reaching out for me, but it worked just as well.

"Micah."

I glanced at him, shielding my eyes from the sun so I could see him sitting there in the shade.

"Thanks for asking," he said. "No one ever asks. Everyone knew we were together. But it's like they're afraid to talk about it. They tell me I'm better off or whatever. But they don't want to know if that's what I think."

"Is it? What you think?"

He shrugged. "I don't know." He smiled his stage smile at me, the one he gave to fans, the one that made people fall in love with him. "But I'm glad you asked."

I nodded, even though I wondered if he was teasing me a little. "Me too." And his expression went sweeter when I said it. I walked back to the bus confused and flustered and strangely happy, as if something good had happened to me. I just wasn't exactly sure if that was right.

chapter two

the next day, when we were on the road again, headed for Toronto, it was Bellamy who sought me out.

I was drawing. It was something I'd done on and off for a while. I wasn't very good at it—it was only a hobby. But Quinn had warned me, when he got me the job, that being on the road, those long hours stuck on the bus, was about the most boring thing imaginable, and he'd been right. He'd told me to bring books or whatever else I could think of to keep myself occupied for a few hours in that enclosed space. I was glad I'd brought the sketchpad and the handful of nice pencils. I'd drawn so much over the past week, I thought I might even be getting better at it.

Tuck had gotten excited when he'd first seen what I was doing. I'd only been drawing objects—the hang of the curtains over the bunks, a guitar propped sideways against a couch, a stack of games at the front of the bus. I hadn't wanted to draw the band without asking, and I'd been too shy to ask. But Tuck thought I was some artistic genius. He'd insisted I draw whoever I wanted, and he'd gotten everybody else to agree. So I'd drawn Ava laughing and Bellamy's hands, resting on his knees, his eyes glued to his book. Tuck and Lissa leaning in toward each other, smiling that secret smile that lovers gave each other when they were totally infatuated. Tuck had started hanging the sketches up, which I found kind of horrifying, but everyone else seemed to like it, or at least tolerate it. Now my pathetic attempts at art littered the front section of the bus. Tuck had taped stuff to the walls between the windows, and then, when he'd started running out of places he liked, moved up, so my drawings hung on the ceiling.

It was weird for me to see them all the time. Made me half-nervous and half-bubbly with a warm feeling I couldn't define. And it made my skin crawl a little, because they were only sketches, and every time I saw them, I saw things I could have done better.

When Bellamy found me, I was tucked into my corner of the couch at the back of the room, out of the way and slightly separate from everyone else, trying hard to ignore the sketches that were already slathered on the walls, and working on a new one.

There wasn't a lot of room on my little stretch of couch, and Bellamy jammed himself right up next to me, so our bodies were touching from knee to hip to shoulder. My first thought was to shy away, because he made me nervous and I couldn't imagine he'd meant to sit so close. But he didn't pull away, and I realized that, as nervous as I was, I didn't want to move.

"Are you drawing?" He didn't lean over me to see, but waited, patient.

I nodded and turned the sketchpad toward him. I was drawing Ava. She was my favorite subject, whether she was at the drum kit, or sitting in front of her games, or walking down the street. Her whole body was always in motion, even when she was seated. Energy hummed from her. She was sitting on the floor now, in front of the TV, with a game controller in her hands. In my sketch, she was leaning far forward, her body almost rising from her spot on the floor, her hands thrust out while she yelled at her character, trying to get him to move where she wanted.

Bellamy laughed, soft, and glanced up at me. "You're good."

The compliment brought a smile to my face. "Thanks."

He gestured at my sketchpad. "Do you draw me?"

I glanced up at the ceiling, and my drawings, all scattered just a few feet above us. "You know I do."

He tapped his fingers on the rings of the pad. "Recently?"

I hesitated, then flipped back a few pages to the drawing I'd done after our last conversation. I hadn't been able to get the image of him—sitting there against the wall, cigarette dangling between his fingers, eyes staring far away—out of my mind. I'd gone back to my bunk, picked up the pencil, and drawn him in hard, dark lines, the whole thing more an impression than a clear picture. I'd drawn his sharp nose and the smooth line of his shoulder, and the flex in his hand. His elbow, pressed to his knees. His hair, just in his eyes.

It wasn't that good. I wasn't under any impressions that drawing was some secret talent I had. But it wasn't completely terrible, either. Bellamy stared at the picture for a long time, until I started wanting to fidget. His hand hovered over the page, like he wanted to touch it. He didn't, though. After a bit, he carefully flipped the pages back and shut the cover, tapping it once with his knuckles. He leaned forward until he could look up into my face. His hair fell into his eyes again, like it had been in the drawing.

"Stop being afraid of me."

"I'm not afraid of you," I said, surprised.

His lips quirked up. "Stop being so afraid to say the wrong thing."

For a second, I let myself close my eyes and be embarrassed. Then I opened them again, and he was still watching me. "I seem to do it a lot, though."

His grin got wider. He sat back and pushed his fingers through his hair. "I like it when you do." I wanted him to touch me again, like he had yesterday.

"And when you change your mind about that?"

He laughed. "See?" His expression mellowed a little, became something gentler, more personal. "I liked talking to you. That's all."

I sighed. "I didn't mean to pry. About your boyfriend and you, and . . ." I hadn't realized, until I'd said it, that it had still been bothering me. But I had never expected to have a conversation like that with him, at all. I'd always imagined what I might say to him, if I got a chance, and poking around into his painful spots was definitely not it. I didn't want him to think I was the type of person who went around doing that. Even if the evidence he had about me so far proved that I did.

"It's fine. I don't . . . I probably said too much." He flashed me a smile, and it was as bright and bold as any he gave on stage, but this close, I thought maybe there was a tiny edge of uncertainty to it as well. "Probably bored you with my whining."

I shook my head. "You didn't. Not at all."

"Good." He stretched the word out, and I could hear the gravelly depth in his voice. "We're good, then?"

I nodded.

"Okay." Another smile. Then he must have decided to have mercy on me, because he stood up. He gave me a tiny bow, the movement perfect and precise and practiced. Graceful, the same as when he was on stage, performing for an audience. I wondered if he was performing for me too, or if he was always performing a bit, no matter where he was, or who he was with.

I was still thinking about Bellamy and the conversations we'd had while I set up Ava's drum kit for sound check that evening, a few hours before the show. When she'd interviewed me—or given me what could be called an interview in terms of getting hired as a roadie by a rock band—she'd hovered over me, watched me pull out each drum and piece of hardware. Some guys would probably have minded, especially since she was a girl and I was expected to cater to her.

I didn't care what gender someone was, though. I'd never seen it have any effect on someone's ability to play an instrument. I'd talked to Ava, and I'd been listening to her play for years. She was no fool, on or off the stage. Even when she was playing video games, which she did nearly every spare minute she spent on the tour bus, she played them with a forceful, dedicated precision, the same kind she used when she drummed. She could hover if she wanted to. She could tell me I was doing everything wrong, and I'd have listened, because she was that good. But she didn't. I had asked her questions, when I'd first met her, about how she liked everything to be, the tuning and the spacing of the kit. She still finalized everything, even now. But now I knew her, and what she wanted. We could set up together and make it go faster, or I could set up for her by myself if she had somewhere else to be.

I liked working with the drums best, because it was what I was used to, what I knew, but I did guitars and pedals and mics too. I was doing the final sound check for the drums and vocals, noodled around on a guitar and listened to drunk people cheer for me like I was the coolest thing ever. Then I got out the set lists and stuck them to the floor, dashed around one more time, made sure everything was perfect, and scooted off to the side of the stage. I liked to stand a tiny bit behind the line of the curtain, where I could see the band in profile, and half the crowd, but no one could see me unless they were really searching for me.

The lights went out. There was always that deep pause, the sharp intake of a thousand breaths in the dark, the swell of anticipation. It was heavy, that excitement. A weight I could feel in my chest, a chain that connected me to every other person in the room. I remembered the first time I'd experienced it from the other side like this. I hadn't been a roadie then. I'd been a drummer in an opening band, first on the stage. The crowd hadn't had a clue who I was. But I'd walked out on stage in the dark, sat down, and picked up my sticks, and I'd felt it. Like magic that clung to my skin. It had been different from being in the audience. Far more nerve-racking. But it had made me feel tingly and powerful and giant too. Like that two-foot gap from the floor to the stage made me a king, if a humble one. I'd been so happy then. So blissfully happy, like I was finally full, complete, like all the hollow spaces inside me had been filled. I'd thought then that I'd never want anything like I wanted to be on the stage, waiting for the lights to come up.

Tuck and Ava went out now, followed a second later by Bellamy, and when the lights rose that little bit, the crowd went nuts. People actually screamed so loud it sounded like it hurt, but I understood it. I'd been one of them, once, screaming for the same band.

On this tour, so far, Escaping Indigo had always opened with the same song. I heard that, along with nearly the same set of songs following it, night after night. I hadn't gotten tired of them, though. I didn't think I ever would. I wasn't standing in the crowd, wasn't getting the wild, surging rush that being with all those people in front of a band I loved gave me. I wasn't looking up at Bellamy while he was on stage, in awe, hoping to catch his eye. It wasn't quite the same, standing off to the side. But it mattered less than I'd thought it would. Seeing them, right there in front of me, watching them play all those songs I knew so well, still filled me with a sparking, fiery electricity. Like the music was getting into my veins, pumping into my heart.

I tried to keep my mouth shut while I watched. While I let my hands roam over guitar strings, tuning, getting them ready for the next song. I knew all the words, but I didn't want Ava or Tuck or Bellamy, especially Bellamy, to glance my way and catch me singing.

I couldn't decide, some nights, whether I was happier knowing them, being the guy who handled their instruments and lived on their bus with them, and watched from the side of the stage, or whether I preferred having been the anonymous fan. Whether I would still rather be that guy in the middle of the crowd, staring up at Bellamy and screaming the lyrics with him, hoping he looked my way and taking comfort in the idea that I could be anything or nothing to him. Wondering if he would notice me. Half fearing that he would or he wouldn't. Being just a fan had sometimes made me feel so far away, so separate, and so desperate to be there myself, in that spot the band occupied. Jealous, almost, of the bands that had made it. I didn't want to take anything away from them. I just wanted a piece of it for myself, sometimes so badly that it ripped through me with an envy and want I couldn't control.

But now, knowing the band even the little bit that I did made things feel almost too close, too personal, and I wasn't sure which was better. When I'd been nothing more than another face in the crowd, I'd harbored that little fantasy of being noticed, being closer to them, but now that it'd actually happened, it didn't seem real. It was hard to make myself remember that it was. That I was part of this now, even if it wasn't in the way I'd always assumed it would be.

I hadn't been lying to Bellamy, when I'd told him I liked being on the road. I did. It had given me something to do, to focus on, when I'd been hollowed out and cast adrift. I liked the instant gratification of it, the simple contentment of a job well done. I was grateful to Quinn—sound guy, roadie, and unofficial manager for Escaping Indigo—for hiring me, because I had no idea what I'd be doing with myself now if he hadn't. Rotting away somewhere, I supposed, and thinking about what might have been.

After the show, Quinn and I, and whatever house help the venue provided, would find ourselves alone on stage for a few minutes. We started to tear down: loading gear, coiling up cords, packing away instruments so they wouldn't be damaged while we traveled. Most nights the band came back after a bit, when the crowds had gone, because they weren't jerks and the job was really meant for more than a couple of people. Ava and I took apart the drum set and packed everything away in its particular case. She always looked drained, tired, but usually she seemed somewhat euphoric too. Floaty. They all did. There wasn't much talk, after a show, at least for that short period of time when we were on the stage together taking things apart, but Tuck and Ava and Bellamy gave off this hum, like all that energy and magic they'd created was still buzzing through them, giving them a kind of glow.

Tuck was about to roll the last guitar case away when Quinn ran over and asked him to wait. He ducked around the side, then clapped Tuck on the shoulder and jogged across the stage to me, a paper flapping in his hand. He handed it to me. It was this night's set list, dated and with the venue name printed on it, that I'd taped to the crate at the start of the show.

"Oh, thanks. I forgot." I'd been collecting them since the first night of the tour. The sets were slightly different, so Quinn gave me a new list for each show so I'd know which guitars to get ready and such. They were similar enough that it was probably foolish to keep them, but I thought of them as some kind of proof. When I'd been on the other side of the stage, I'd been the kid reaching up, hoping to take a set list home with me, to remember, to hold on to as tangible evidence that I'd been there, seen this incredible, amazing thing. Now they did the same thing for me, told me that this had been real, from the other side of the stage. Proved that I had been a part of this. I needed that, craved it, needed to hold on to the idea that I was here, that this was happening. That my life hadn't stopped with the end of my music career and everything else.

Quinn must have seen that I was collecting them. It surprised me that he'd noticed. Before I could say anything else to him, though, he was already turning away, gathering the house help and thanking them before we headed out.

I folded the paper carefully and slipped it into my back pocket. When I looked up, Bellamy was watching me. His face was blank, and for a second I wasn't even sure he was seeing me at all. Then he blinked, and I realized he'd been watching me put the set list away. He met my eyes, and for a heartbeat his expression stayed the same—as if he was trying to figure something out. Or something was only now occurring to him. Then he smiled, a bit smug, before he turned away.

When Quinn and I finished packing everything away, we went up the steps of the bus and found the band there. They hadn't spread out, like they usually did when we sat in the bus, separated into our own personal spaces. Instead, they were sprawled all over each other. They sometimes did that after a show. It was as if the last barriers between them broke down after they played music together. Tuck and Bellamy sat on the couch, Tuck's arm around Bellamy's shoulders, Bellamy leaning into him. Ava was lounging on the floor at Tuck's feet, one hand on Bellamy's knee, so anyone who wanted to get by would have to step over her. Bellamy's other foot was tapping an unsteady beat out against the floor, as if he didn't realize he was doing it. Ava kept patting his knee as if she was soothing him, but I wasn't sure he noticed. He'd stop for a second, and then start back up again, like he wasn't quite in control. Lissa sat across from them, an indulgent smile on her face. The band wasn't paying us much attention, though. They were focused inward.

I stepped past, said good night, not sure if anyone heard me, and headed for my bunk.

I ducked into the bathroom and brushed my teeth, took off my clothes, and tugged on a pair of pajama pants. I pulled the set list from the pocket of my jeans, unfolded it, and slipped it into a pocket in the back of my sketchbook with the others. Then I tucked the book and my clothes into the little cubby beside the bunks. My own bunk was the second one up of three, and I did a little hop and jumped into it, not bothering with the ladder built into the side. I was reaching to pull the curtains closed when Bellamy appeared, leaning his head in, arms folded on my mattress. He raised one hand in a tiny wave, and I thought I saw his fingers shake, some excess of energy still trickling through him.

"Hey."

I raised my eyebrows. "Hey."

I didn't know what he was doing here. This was the second time he'd sought me out, and it was something he hadn't done at all before. I couldn't figure out why he was doing it. Decently famous rock star wants, for some reason, the attention of the lowly roadie. It was enough to make me want to laugh, if I hadn't wanted it to be true so badly.

He settled his chin on his hands, almost as if he was using the weight to keep them still, and his eyes drifted closed. A small shiver raced through him, making his shoulders twitch, and he took a deep breath, and then another, and another, like he was coming down from something. As if he had been out of breath and he was only now catching it. I took a second to stare at him while he wasn't watching me do it. His fingers were all calloused, and he had little scrapes on the back of his hand, like he'd rubbed up against a brick wall or something. I could see all the fine lines around his eyes, the spots that might be wrinkles from laughter later in life. He only seemed tired and worn now, though. Not sleepy so much as . . . drained. Like he'd left everything he had out on the stage. He didn't look unhappy or uncomfortable—he had a bit of that content glow I could see so clearly on Ava and Tuck after a show, buried underneath. It just didn't make him look less exhausted.

"Bellamy," I said softly. I could hear the others moving around at the front of the bus, but it seemed that Bellamy and I were in a private bubble. "Are you okay? Do you want to go to bed?"

He opened his eyes. "Can't. Too wired."

I wasn't sure *wired* was the word I'd have used, but I didn't argue. "Do you want . . ." I hesitated, not sure if I should ask. So what if he'd paid me a bit of attention? It didn't mean anything in the long run. If he wanted someone to talk to, he had the rest of the band, or even Lissa or Quinn. They'd all known him longer than I had. But he'd come over here. He'd come to my bunk. "Do you want to come sit with me for a while?"

He hesitated and then nodded. I tucked my knees in and my feet under, making room for him. The bunks were spacious, but two people in one was probably asking a lot. I dug my toes into the sheets, trying to make myself smaller.

Bellamy hauled himself up, and I clicked on the little reading lamp in the wall. He sat opposite me, mirroring my pose, all tucked up and contained, arms wrapped around his knees. I looked at him while he looked at me, his face oddly sharpened by the soft light. His eyes were dark, but the light caught the highlights in them, the hazel and gold in the deep brown. Made them sparkle like they did when he was on stage.

I reached out to close the curtain, giving us the illusion of privacy, and he leaned his head back against the wall, tipping a bit sideways, and closed his eyes. He was breathing deeply, but it didn't seem calm.

"I can never be sure," he said, eyes still closed, "if we're doing okay. It was a good show, right?" That thread of tension in his body had made its way into his voice. He wrapped his arms even tighter around his knees.

I didn't know what to say. I couldn't believe he was asking *me*. He must have known it was a good show. There was no way he couldn't. The crowd had been wild for him.

"It was perfect." I couldn't quite keep the incredulity out of my voice. "You're always perfect."

His lips lifted at the corners, halfway between a smile and a grimace, and he opened his eyes to see me. "There, you're wrong. I am definitely not always perfect."

I swallowed. I'd never heard him talk this way. Had never expected it. "Okay. But why would you think it wasn't good?"

He shook his head, the movement tiny and fast. "I just can't tell. I'll go over it in my mind . . . over and over. But I can't tell if I'm remembering right. I can't remember if I messed up, or if I did mess up, I can't remember how bad it was. I don't know what people see, when I'm up there on stage. I can't tell." His breathing was picking up again as he spoke.

"You were fine," I said, trying to go for a soothing tone. I was getting a bit panicked myself. I didn't know why he was thinking these things. It must only have been because he was tired. Because he was too exhausted to think straight. "Better than fine. I've never seen a band play the way you do on stage. You're all amazing. Bellamy. Are you really okay?"

He blinked and straightened up, tipping his shoulders back. "I'm fine. Thanks. I'm glad."

I nodded. I didn't know if I'd said the right thing, if I should say or ask something else, or let it go. He looked like he was trying to focus, like he was pulling himself out of his own thoughts, out of his memories of the show. He shoved a hand through his hair, hard, and then dropped it into his lap. For a second, we stared at each other in the near dark, and a different tension, something sweet and unnameable and frightening, grew between us.

He leaned forward a little, but then he froze. "What's that?" He pointed down at my side.

I clapped a hand to my skin, over the left side of my waist. "Nothing." My face started to burn as soon as I said it, because who ever expected that answer to be believed? I wasn't even really sure why I was hiding it. Automatic response.

"That's my band." He moved forward again, and reached out to pry my hand away. He lifted my wrist to the side and stared at the black and purple drawing over my hip. "You've got my band tattooed on you."

"Yes. I do." I pressed my lips together, hard.

I waited for him to tease me, but he didn't. He glanced up at me, his eyes shadowed by his lashes and the hair falling in his face. He reached up to brush it back, and his hand was trembling again, a slight tremor that made him seem a tiny bit unsteady, unsettled. "Why?"

"I like the emblem."

He grinned and sat back. "You do not."

I shook my head, a laugh bubbling up at how absolutely incredulous his expression was. "I like the band, Bellamy." I liked the emblem too. I wouldn't have tattooed it on myself if I didn't. But it was Escaping Indigo that was the real reason.

Bellamy's back thumped against the end of the bunk. "You were a fan."

"Yeah." I felt even more foolish that I'd covered the tattoo with my hand, but in that second, I hadn't wanted him to see. I hadn't wanted him to think of me as that ever-changing, ever-present face in the crowd. I hadn't wanted him to see me the way he saw every other fan out there. Stupid of me to walk around without a shirt on, then. I just hadn't thought of it until he'd gone to touch it.

"Since when?" He sounded almost suspicious, but eager too.

"Since forever," I admitted. I had them tattooed on me—seemed silly to deny how much I loved them now that he'd seen it. "Since the first single. I heard it in my car." I swallowed. "I sat in my driveway and listened. My dad came out and asked me what was wrong, I sat there so long."

Bellamy smiled. It was an introspective smile, as if he was picturing it. "We were just kids then. When that song came out."

I did laugh then, surprising us both a little. "You're still a kid, Bellamy."

He tipped his head to the side. "I'm twenty-six, Micah."

I nodded. I'd been sixteen the first time I heard his voice. I was twenty-two now. That seemed young, I suppose—both of our ages did—but for musicians, for people trying to succeed in a band, we were hitting our expiration dates. And most days, for me, twenty-two didn't feel young. It was if, instead, I'd grown up and hadn't seen it happening. Like the whole world was moving except for me. Sometimes I thought I was stuck and couldn't catch up to where I was supposed to be, and it made me feel too old and too young at the same time, left behind and out of time. "Still."

He smiled again. It was a small thing that looked almost hesitant on his face. "Are you still a fan?"

I nodded. I wanted to cover the tattoo with my palm again, or run my fingers over it, feel the raised skin, heavy with ink. Instead, I bunched my fingers in the bed covers, kneading the fabric.

"Is that why you kept the set list?"

I gave a half shrug. "I want to remember."

He nodded as if that made sense, but he asked, "Do you think you're going to forget?" He huffed out a short laugh. "Do you think you won't remember being on tour with us?"

I shook my head and smiled back, but it was a wobbly smile, because sometimes I was afraid. Sometimes I woke up in the middle of the night with my heart pounding, scared that I was losing time, that I'd forgotten something important, that I'd lost more than I'd realized and now I couldn't get it back. I didn't honestly think I'd forget that I'd been here with Escaping Indigo, with Bellamy and Quinn and the others, that I'd seen them play each night, seen them be such shining, beautiful rock stars. Or that I'd spent all these quieter hours with them, either, while we drove from place to place, while we set up and tore down. But sometimes I worried that it would feel like a dream, that I would wonder if it had all been in my head.

"I want to remember that it was real," I said.

He reached out to touch my side, his fingers skimming over the tattoo. I wanted to shiver at his touch, wanted to lean into him, let him press his hand against me. I made myself stay still. "Does that make sense?"

He nodded, his eyes still focused on his fingers against me, the swirls of the design on my skin. "It's real, Micah. I don't think you're going to forget that. But I like that you keep the set lists." He pulled his hand away and looked up at me. "Why didn't you say anything? Didn't tell me you were a fan?"

I wiggled my toes until they were under the covers. He didn't turn away from me, and I wondered if I could just wiggle myself right off the bunk. I met his eyes, though, and I didn't think he was laughing at me. He didn't seem smug, knowing that I'd liked his band enough to tattoo them on me. He only seemed curious.

"What would you have said? 'Thanks'?" I shrugged. He kept his eyes on me. "I'd be . . . one of thousands. I didn't want . . . I wanted you to see me as me. All of you. I didn't want to be faceless." It was selfish, and cruel. I knew it was wrong—the fans were important, and they certainly weren't all mindless groupies. I had been a fan, just a fan, no matter what I was now, and I hadn't been mindless at all. But I'd thought if he knew that, that was all he'd ever see of me.

Bellamy was shaking his head. "It never gets old, you know. To have someone tell you they like what you do. It won't ever, I don't think. It always takes me by surprise. Something like that—" He pointed at my side. "I can't believe you like us enough to do that. I would have wanted to know."

I nodded, uncomfortable, and pulled my knees closer to my chest. "I'll tell you, next time."

He laughed. He still sounded tired. But not quite as worn, maybe, as before. "Okay. It's a promise, then. Micah, can I ask you something?"

I nodded, and he swept his hand through his hair like he was trying to figure out how to phrase something. "This whole being nervous with me thing—is it because of that? Because I think you are, I can feel it when we talk. Is it because you're a fan of the music?"

I wasn't sure whether to shake my head or nod. "You're . . . you. Bellamy. Rock star. Larger than life."

For a second, only a second, he looked completely lost, as if I'd crushed him with those few words. He drew his knees up, wrapped his arms around them, gathering himself in. "I'm not, though."

I traced around my own kneecap with a finger, just wanting something to do with my hands. I watched my finger move so I wouldn't have to meet his gaze. "Okay."

He sighed, and I glanced up to see him pressing his lips together. "Look. You can think whatever you want. But I'm not . . . I'm not built like everyone else." He ran his hand through his hair again, frustrated. "That's not what I meant to say."

I smiled. I felt shy and awkward. Maybe this hadn't been a good idea after all. "I know you're not like everyone else. That's the whole point."

He dropped his hand and shook his head. "No. I mean, I'm the opposite of what you think. I'm not larger than life. I'm . . ." He took a deep breath, and for a second, something flashed across his face. Fear or doubt, some emotion he couldn't control and, for that moment, couldn't hide.

"Bellamy." I reached out without thinking and caught his hand. We both stared at it, my fingers around his, and I wanted to take it back, but I was too frozen to do it. I looked up at him. "Are you okay?" I asked again.

He nodded. "Yes. For now, I'm okay."

I didn't quite believe him. There was something there, something else. It seemed like he'd pulled back the curtain of himself, just a little. I had always thought he was bigger and better than me in a thousand ways. I still did. I didn't think I'd be able to shake that very easily. But here, in the dark and the quiet, there was something so human and tender about him, something that made me want to ask him to tell me what it was, what was worrying him.

I didn't, though. I nodded and let go of his hand.

"I should go," he said. He wasn't quite meeting my eyes, and I wondered how we'd gotten here, to this weird, awkward place.

"Bellamy," I said, to grab his attention. It was stupid, and I didn't know what I wanted to say, but I didn't want him to leave with all this tension floating between us. "You can tell me stuff. If you want to. I won't . . . I can listen. I'm good at that."

He smiled, but it was an unbalanced expression that told me, before he even said a word, that he was going to brush me off. And it made me feel sad and a bit small.

"Thank you." He sounded so sincere, but he didn't offer up anything else. I told myself that I wasn't disappointed, that I didn't need him to tell me anything else, because we were basically still strangers and he didn't owe me anything. But I wished he felt like he could, if he wanted to, and it was obvious he didn't. I tried not to let that sting, but it was hard.

Maybe he saw something of that on my face, because he leaned forward, fast, and brushed a kiss over my cheek. The kiss lingered a little, enough that I could feel the shape of his mouth on my skin, his hand against my knee where he was bracing himself. Could feel when he breathed in.

"Thank you," he said again as he leaned back. Then he pulled the curtain aside, hopped down, and disappeared into his own bunk. And I did my damnedest not to lift my hand to my face and touch the spot he'd kissed.

chapter three

X

the next show was in Boston, and afterward, we all got drunk. None of us were usually into that—the band didn't seem much into throwing crazy parties with groupies, or partying like there was no tomorrow, and then spending the wee hours of the morning huddled together over the tiny bus toilet. I'd almost expected it—rock stars have a certain reputation—but I hadn't gotten it, and was glad for the most part. Quinn, Bellamy, and I smoked. I thought Tuck and Lissa indulged in some pot, occasionally, if someone was selling, but that was it. Wine with dinner, if we went out and wanted to pretend we were actually adults. Ava called it "getting fancy."

But that night, Bellamy was different after the show ended and he came off the stage. He paced around in the backstage area for a while. Tuck came over and handed him a water bottle, and made him sit down to drink it. They had a rapid conversation where it looked like Bellamy was trying not to yell at Tuck, and Tuck talked as calmly as possible, which only seemed to set Bellamy off more. As soon as he was done with the water, he handed the empty bottle back to Tuck and went back on stage to start packing up, even though not all of the fans had quite left yet.

I went out on stage a minute later. Bellamy was standing below, where the audience would normally be. A couple of fans, people I assumed he'd been talking to, were walking away, huge grins on their faces. Bellamy watched them leave, and then turned and climbed up to sit on the edge of the stage. He slumped forward, elbows on his knees, and dropped his head into his hands.

I glanced behind me. Quinn was busy with one of the house stagehands, coiling cords and rolling amps across the floor. He caught my eye, looked briefly to Bellamy, then shrugged. Not in a dismissive way, but in a way that told me maybe this wasn't unusual. Or that I shouldn't worry.

I *was* a bit worried, though. Quinn had everything under control for the moment, so I went over and sat next to Bellamy.

He picked his head up as soon as I did, and faced me. He smiled, but the expression looked thin, see-through, like maybe it was a bit of a struggle. He was breathing fast, like he'd been running.

"Did you sign something for those people?" I asked.

He nodded. "Yeah. I . . . They were still here when I came out."

"That was nice."

Another nod. "I don't usually do that. It's not that I don't want to. It's just . . ." He waved his hand around. "I'm pretty . . . done, by the end of a show."

"Good done or bad done?" I said before I could think about exactly what I was poking at, or why.

For a second he stared at me, like he was trying to figure me out. Then he shrugged. "Both. Just . . . it's a lot. It's wonderful. But it's a lot."

I nodded back. I almost got that. Playing a show had always been a boost for me. A spike in energy, like I was flying, like I was electrified. It had been intense.

"Is anyone watching us? Staring?" he asked suddenly. His eyes were a little too wide, but he was focused on my face. He didn't turn to look behind us.

I did and shook my head. "No. It's okay. No one's watching."

He breathed out and slumped a bit more. I didn't know what was going on in his mind. Why he'd be so stressed or embarrassed. It looked almost like a miniature panic attack. Except I'd never seen a panic attack in real life, so I figured I was probably overreacting. But I hadn't expected Bellamy to ever act like this, either. He always seemed so confident and put together.

"Bellamy?" I put my hand on his shoulder, felt how strained his muscles were under my palm.

"I'm fine," he said, his voice hard and a tiny bit breathless at the same time. "I need to come down. That's all."

He didn't shake my hand off, so I didn't move away. I wasn't sure what to do, at all. I wasn't sure if he still wanted me there. But he wasn't asking me to leave, so I was going to stay.

After a few minutes, his breathing slowed, and some of the tension went out of him. I was about to suggest we go back to the bus when Tuck came up and sat on his other side.

"I think we should celebrate," he said without preamble. He leaned forward so he could grin at both me and Bellamy.

"What are we celebrating?" I asked.

"We made it through five shows. No one kicked us off the stage. That calls for celebration." He grinned even wider.

"I think it's been seven shows," I started, but Tuck shushed me in a loud, obvious way, and Bellamy laughed. Dry and sharp and a bit strained, but definitely a laugh. That was enough for me. I grinned back at Tuck and we nodded, and after we finished packing everything up, Tuck made arrangements with Ava. The two of them made a run to the closest liquor store and came back loaded down with whiskey and vodka, and a bottle of white wine for Lissa. Then we sat around on the bus floor and put it away.

We did it a sip at a time, passing bottles and cups, talking and laughing and teasing each other into one more drink. By the time the alcohol was really working on me, I was comfortable, my body melting into its crooked spot against the bottom of the couch, and I was feeling mushy and lovey, thinking that maybe Escaping Indigo and Lissa and Quinn were the best people ever. I'd always been a sentimental drunk.

"We should go out," Bellamy announced from his sprawl across from me. The tension from before was gone, washed away by the time he'd had to himself after the show, and the alcohol. I'd been worried, because I was pretty sure alcohol was a depressant, and I was concerned with how he'd be in the morning, but for now he seemed to be feeling no pain, like the rest of us. He was stretched out so one of his feet bumped into my sneaker and the other was nudging Quinn in the hip. Quinn didn't seem to notice.

"Out where?" Tuck perked up a bit. He fished around for his cup and took another sip.

Bellamy waved his hand through the air. "Out."

"Nowhere public," Quinn mumbled. I wasn't sure when the band had become his responsibility—if they'd hired him to do that job, or if he'd just slowly taken on every aspect of band manager and leader that he could—but it had, and he kept them all safe and relatively intact. Even when he was probably too drunk to do much about anyone's actions but his own. "Nowhere with traffic."

Bellamy nodded, serious. "No traffic." He hauled himself up, pushing with his hands, only wobbling a little, then reached down and scooped Ava up. She let herself be lifted, then turned around and yanked at me until I was standing too. I was glad she kept hold of my hand. Everything was kind of swimmy.

I didn't know where Bellamy planned to go in the dead of night, in a city that none of us were more than cursorily familiar with. Or almost none of us—Ava was from this part of the country, but she'd said she hadn't spent much time in Boston. But we all followed him, let him lead us out of the bus and down the road, sticking to quieter sidewalks—keeping his promise to stay out of traffic—until we reached a park.

I figured we were all about to get arrested for being drunk and disorderly in a public place. I started having flashes of what it would be like to be hungover in a jail cell, and I almost turned back, but Bellamy pulled on my hand. He led us around dark gardens, along twisting paths, like he was looking for something. We hit a stretch of grass and trees, and he slowed down like he'd stop, but then he picked his head up and started tugging me along even faster. There was a small playground ahead of us, and Bellamy was aiming toward it as if getting to it was his greatest mission in life.

He dropped my hand when we got a short way from it, and made a mad dash to the short fence that surrounded it. It took him a minute to boost himself over, but he did it, and we all followed suit, even though I was pretty much dead sure at this point that we shouldn't be there. Bellamy launched himself to the top of the slide, climbing up it backward, and then stood at the pinnacle. He swayed, and I wondered, distantly and in a bit of an alcoholic haze, if he was going to tip. Ava had climbed up the ladder behind him, though, and she slapped a hand firmly onto his backside, balancing him. He turned around, very carefully, and made a surprisingly graceful bow at her.

She bowed awkwardly from the ladder, and I laughed loudly. They both turned to stare at me like I was the one who was crazy.

Tuck flung himself up next to Bellamy, and without any cue or signal that I could see, they both burst into an a cappella cover of a song by another band. And I found that I wasn't laughing anymore. I was captivated. I swayed with the rhythm of the song, and I knew I should probably stop, but I couldn't.

Bellamy glanced down at me and caught my eye, and I felt like I had all those times I'd seen him on stage, when I'd bought tickets and gone to see Escaping Indigo. Those rare moments while he'd been singing, when he'd looked right at me, and for a second we'd been connected. Even though he hadn't known who I was. Even though we'd been strangers. We were still almost strangers now, but not quite. As our eyes met, it was different. Just as thrilling. Just as special. But more intense, and more . . . private, in a way, even though we weren't alone. I kept watching him, and he kept singing, and I wanted the song to go on forever so I could keep standing here, listening to him and Tuck.

Tuck and Bellamy finished the song, had a quiet, almost sober discussion, and then Tuck counted out a quick beat and they started one of their own songs. It was an old one, one they hadn't played at any of the shows this tour, a deeper cut off an album. Bellamy didn't watch me while he sang this time, and maybe it was better, because I couldn't take my eyes off him. There weren't any lights on him, no band to back him, no crowd to cheer him on, no real stage to elevate him. Only Tuck, singing behind him. Both of their voices were rough, and the sound drifted a bit on the thin night air, but it was one of the best things I'd ever seen, ever heard. Stripped down, simple and gorgeous. Raw and real, and I thought I could see, in this, in this song, why they both did what they did, why they'd worked so hard to be musicians. I could almost see it lifting Bellamy up. He was still a rock star, still magic, like he'd glow if I studied him closely enough, even without stage lighting or an audience in front of him, adoring him. It was hard to remember that he'd also been the person overwhelmed by things this afternoon, who had needed to calm down after the show. But staring up at him in the dark, listening to him sing his song, the words he'd written, maybe it wasn't so hard to reconcile that.

Maybe it made sense, because someone who was together and confident and perfect all the time couldn't have written the things that Bellamy had written. But I was glad he was happy and easy now. This had been a good idea of Tuck's.

When the song ended, Bellamy bowed again, a silly gesture, pulling at Tuck until he bowed with him. Ava and Quinn and Lissa clapped, and after a second, I joined in. I felt like I was in a waking dream. I didn't know if it was the drinks or the complete unreality of where I was, who I was with. I felt like I was in someone else's life, and I wanted to stay here.

Bellamy sat and slid the short distance to the ground, and I shook myself. He bounded off with Ava, and the two of them rolled around in the grass like puppies until he had to scramble up in a hurry to eject some of the whiskey he'd had into an unlucky bush. Quinn put an end to our outing then, rounding us up and shuffling us home, nagging us all the way there to drink water when we got back to the bus, even as he slurred a few of his own words.

I found my hand in Bellamy's again as we walked back, and I couldn't remember how it happened. I wasn't sure he even noticed. He swung me around while he talked to everyone else, but he never let go, his grip almost too tight. He pulled me all the way to his own bunk on the bus, then slipped in and closed the curtain without another word. I stood in the hallway, a little confused and a little bit thrilled, until Lissa bumped into me and Tuck told me to get into bed before I fell over.

I thought that in the morning it would be like a dream, that everything would mush and blend together and go foggy. But it didn't. I showered and washed the scents of the night off my skin, but I couldn't get the image of Bellamy, standing over me, singing, staring at me, out of my mind.

chapter four

X

"You want a new head on this tom?" I held up the drum from my spot on the floor. The head must have been left over from before the tour started. It was beat to hell, marked black in the middle, and dented with a hundred tiny divots from where Ava had smacked her sticks against it. Ava glanced at me, glanced at the tom, and nodded.

We were setting up for our eighth gig of the tour, in New York City. Ava was tuning the snare. I was pretty sure that she had actually twisted the head into such submission that it would never consider falling out of tune ever again, but she liked to tweak until she had no more time left. It was a nervous habit more than anything, I thought, and not a particularly useful one, but I supposed it was a lot better than what other musicians sometimes got up to. I took the tom into my lap and started taking the lugs off.

"So how do you know Quinn?" Ava asked. I looked up at her, then back down at the snare. "He was pretty adamant that you were the man for the job."

I smiled and pulled the old head off. I had another in a box, waiting to go, and slid it out and seated it on the drum, pushing it down to make sure it fit without any gaps. The glue crackled. "Maybe because it takes you all day to change a drum head, and me fifteen minutes."

Ava laughed. "Shut up." She set down her drum key and swiveled the throne around so she could see me. "Just curious. You don't have to answer." But she was still staring at me, like the option not to answer should make me want to answer all the more. With anyone else, it might have made me clam up, but Ava was so guileless. I smiled at her.

"Quinn's brother Eric was my best friend growing up. I was his drummer in pretty much every band he ever had. So I guess I had an in."

"Oh." Her short hair bobbed around her face, strands brushing her cheeks. "But you're not in a band with him now."

I nodded, like it was all good. Just a thing that had happened. Or not happened. Normal. "Yeah, no, Eric, um, died." I couldn't keep my voice from rising up at the end of the sentence, like I was asking her a question. The way I put it was too blunt, but I'd never figured out a better way to say it. People would say he'd passed, or that we'd lost him, or that he'd moved on, but all of it was only a pretty way to explain something that was awful. I'd rather tell it like it was. I felt bad saying it that way, though. I stared back down at the drum I was holding, at the lugs I was placing back into their spots. They twisted in my hands, suddenly slippery, the metal too hot against my fingertips.

"What?" She stood, as if it was too much to process sitting down. "He what?"

I stared up at her. "Yeah, overdose . . ." Then it finally dawned on me that she hadn't known, at all. That Quinn hadn't told her, maybe hadn't told any of them, even though he was their friend, had been working with them for a long time. And I'd just blurted it out, like I was ripping off a Band-Aid. I put the drum down and stood, reached out a hand for her. "Yeah. Look, I guess maybe Quinn doesn't want to talk about it? So if you could not mention it . . ."

She grabbed for the throne and slumped down onto it, her shoulders collapsing in, hands between her knees. "Jesus." She looked at me. "So he got you the job because you were his brother's friend."

I didn't think it was exactly like that. I thought it had had less to do with my relationship with Eric, and more to do with the guilt Quinn carried around, about Eric and about me, for not being there or whatever when Eric had needed him. When I'd needed help with Eric. Which was bullshit. Eric had done it to himself, and I wished that wasn't true, that it hadn't happened, but I didn't kid myself into thinking that Quinn's hanging around could have made things turn out differently, either.

"And because you're good," she added. I focused on her again and saw her watching me, a faint smile on her lips. She looked sorry, but not pitying.

I smiled back at her. It felt fragile on my face, an expression that would crack under the lightest pressure. "Please don't tell him you know, Ava. I shouldn't have said anything."

"Okay. But he was your best friend. You get to decide who knows what you're going through as much as anyone."

I nodded and kept smiling, even though it seemed like the completely wrong expression for this conversation. "Thank you. But, please—"

She held up a hand, then let it flop down. "Don't worry. Secret's safe."

"Thanks." I sat back down, pulled the tom into my lap. I tightened the lugs by hand first, twisting them in my fingers until I couldn't tighten them anymore. Then I picked up my drum key and started really tuning, a twist at a time. I paused, tapped at the drum, listening to the tone, then twisted the lugs again. There was a certain ritual in tuning, and it was soothing, almost. Something I could focus on.

"Were you good?" Ava asked after a few minutes. I glanced up. "Your band?"

I reminded myself to breathe in. "Pretty good."

"What about the other people in your band? Where are they? Did they . . . Did you not want to be in a band with them anymore?"

I shrugged. "I stay in touch with a couple people we played with," I said, avoiding what she was really asking. "But it was always me and Eric at the heart of things. We played in a lot of bands. Put a lot of bands together. But Eric and I . . ." Eric had been my best friend. Those other guys were cool, and I didn't mind getting together with them once in a while, but we didn't play music together anymore, and they didn't feel Eric's loss like I did. They just didn't.

Ava let it go at that, and I was glad, because I didn't want to say anything more about it. Not then. We finished putting the kit together. It didn't take long, and we didn't talk much for the rest of it, but it wasn't uncomfortable. When we were done, Ava went to hand me the huge black cover we flung over her drum set, to keep it out of sight and in the background until she was ready to go on. But she tugged it back at the last second and looked at the drum set, then at me.

"D'you wanna play?" she asked, her words all tumbling together.

I followed the same line her gaze had taken, to the kit and back. "Would you mind?"

She shook her head. "You haven't played since we've been on tour, right? You'll get rusty."

I probably should have told her it wouldn't matter. There wasn't any band for me to go back to. If I got rusty, I'd have all the time in the world to clean up my skills when I got home, and no one but me would care anyway. But I stared at the kit again, at the dark wood, stained flat black, the silver rims on the drums, the heavy hardware, the rough finish on the coated heads. Ava touched my elbow.

"No one's here but you. Just put everything back when you're done."

I nodded. "Thank you."

I had my bag backstage, and I pulled my headphones and iPod out. The headphones weren't your standard earbuds, but professional headphones that blocked external noise, so I could hear my songs even while I played. I'd still have to crank the music, but it'd be worth it. I sat at the kit and put them on. Instantly, everything was muffled. I couldn't hear any stray conversations from the front of the building, couldn't hear the hiss of the air conditioner, couldn't even hear my feet moving over the pedals, my hand flicking the snares on. My hearing, my focus, went inward. My heartbeat was loud in my chest. When I swallowed, the sound echoed through me.

It was weird to sit behind drums again. Even though it had only been a couple weeks, the space felt foreign. I had to raise the throne so I fit, and I'd have adjusted the snare too, if the microphones weren't already in place—Ava was much shorter than me. It was more than that, though. I'd kept playing, eventually, even after Eric had died, but it had been different then, too. It had felt like knowing that no matter what happened from then on, I'd always be playing for a different reason, a different outcome, a different goal. It would never be the same. And it still wasn't. I'd had a path, before, when I'd sat behind a kit and made music. I'd had somewhere to drive the music *to*. And now I didn't. The fact that not having that deliberate, strict path felt almost good made me even more nervous than the path itself ever had.

It was still comfortable too, though, a familiarity I wasn't sure I'd ever get anywhere else. The sticks were slightly heavy in my hands, but balanced. I made a round of the toms, a quick, simple run of fills and an easy pattern to get a feel for the set. Then I leaned down and turned my music on.

I stared out at the dark theater in front of me, listening to the opening of the song, waiting for the drums to come in. I tried to imagine what it was like for Ava every night, to sit there and stare out past the lights, into the shadows, and know that there were thousands of people there, watching her, listening to her play. There *for her*. I'd played gigs before. I'd done my own share of shows. No band I'd been in had drawn a crowd like that, though. Eric and I had come close. We'd been crawling our way toward that. We just hadn't quite gotten there.

I looked back down at the off-white drum heads, marked silvery black in a few places where Ava had struck them the night before, the coating slowly wearing away. I tried to focus on them and the drums and the pedals. I tried to forget where I was.

I let myself play three songs. I wasn't going to do more than that—one as a warm-up, to make me remember how it felt to be a drummer. One that was fast and hard and heavy, to make the blood pump, to make my hands and feet tingly and warm, to make my heart pound. And one to be creative with, to play over, to test out a few fills on. I could have kept going, could have played and played. I wanted to sit there and play and not think, for a long time. I knew I'd get lost in it, though, and there wasn't time for that. This wasn't the place. It was generous that Ava had offered me her kit at all.

Instead, I let myself fall, for those few minutes, into the music. Let myself drift into the pocket of the songs—it had taken me so long to figure that out, what the pocket was. A term thrown around by guys who wanted to seem like better players than they were, I'd always thought, and for the most part, it was true. But when you hit it, when you were actually there, it was as if the music were coming up to meet you, as if you'd slipped into the very center of it. Found not only the rhythm and the beat, but the heart of the song, and become part of it. It was the thing I loved most about drumming. Being in the center like that. Holding everything together. Waiting until that exact right nanosecond to hit the snare or the bass drum, and having it be easy. Feeling it and hearing it and knowing I'd done it right. It was so incredibly, wonderfully, startlingly good.

Then the last song ended, and I was done. I put the sticks back, shut off my music, took off the headphones. I wanted more. My fingers ached for it. But I couldn't let myself have it, not right now.

I lowered the seat again, then walked around the kit, making sure everything was exactly as it should be. The only thing I'd moved was the throne, and there'd be another quick sound check before Escaping Indigo went on anyway, but I wanted to double-check. I wanted to spend more time pretending that it was my kit. That it was me, about to go on stage. That Eric would stand in front of me and we would play music together, and I wouldn't be so adrift and confused without him, without our band, without sticks in my hands.

I moved around the kit for a while afterward, even though there wasn't anything else for me to do. I just liked seeing it, with all its dull gleam, the matte black of the finish, the copper of the cymbals, tuned and ready and waiting.

Being in a band was a heady thing. I knew what music, songs, bands, had done for me. I knew how they'd shaped me, changed me, made me think and feel in ways I never would have before. I knew what a force music could be, what a powerful thing. When I'd made music with Eric, that had always been in my mind. That we had a responsibility to do our best, to try our hardest, to live up to the bands that had come before us. I didn't know if anyone else thought that way, or if I was the only neurotic one, wondering what people were taking away from the music we offered. I didn't know if even Eric had seen things like that. He'd been enslaved to the music, while I'd been enslaved to what the music could do. I supposed that'd been part of the reason why we'd worked well together, why we'd been best friends. We'd complemented each other, filled in the spaces where the other needed support. We'd fit together.

I went back to the bus by myself. It was quiet. Tuck had an interview with a local radio station that afternoon, but I had no idea where anyone else had gone. I didn't care. I was worn out from playing—not only the physical aspect of it, but the way it felt so familiar and so strange at the same time. And talking about Eric always left me feeling raw. I always imagined that it would get easier, that after I told this person, or the next, I'd get used to it. That the stabbing feeling inside me that echoed around in the hollow where Eric had been would be less. But it never was. Instead, it made it all seem like it had happened yesterday, not eight months ago. It would hit me all over again. And it was funny, because when I was lost like that, when everything hurt and I was scared and in pain, my first thought was still to turn to Eric. It was then that I needed the most to call him, talk to him, have him beside me. I needed to hear his voice, needed to hear him talking about music or books or what he had for dinner, anything, in that calm, reserved way of his that told me everything was okay. And when my brain caught up with my heart, and I remembered that I could never have that again, it hurt so much worse.

I wanted to sleep. I wanted to lie down and forget that any of this was happening, lose myself in dreams for an hour or two, until the pain went away enough that I could focus. I'd slept a lot, right after Eric died. I hadn't known what else to do with myself. It had been Quinn who'd told me I had to stop doing that. I'd been living in the apartment over the garage at his mom's house—still would live there, when I went home. I'd answered the door to his knock one afternoon, still in my pajamas, hair crazy and dirty, eyes red. I'd been weak, all my muscles as tired as my heart, because I hadn't been moving, and most of the time, I'd been forgetting to eat. Quinn had taken one look at me, slumped against the doorframe, and completely lost his shit at me. He'd told me I could get my act together and stop sleeping all fucking day, or I was out.

Quinn was Eric's brother, but we weren't exactly friends. I'd figured it wouldn't cost him much to kick me out. I'd gotten myself together. I'd gone back to work, and I'd set my drum kit up again, although it had taken me a long time to actually sit down behind it. And now, when I wanted to sleep to escape, I forced myself to do something else. So instead of crawling into my bunk and pulling the curtain now, I reached in and grabbed the paperback I'd been reading. Then I headed for the curtained-off room at the back of the bus. I wasn't going to sleep through the afternoon, but that didn't mean I wanted to chitchat with everyone when they came back from wherever they were, either.

I pulled aside the curtain, and Bellamy was there.

My first thought was to duck right back out. I wasn't sure what was going on with me and Bellamy. It almost seemed like he'd been trying to get to know me, but I figured that was more a socially demanded nicety than anything. I didn't figure he actually wanted me bursting in on him and hanging around. He'd probably come back here for the same privacy I was hoping for.

I wasn't sure I wanted to be around him right now, either.

I couldn't help staring at him. He didn't look like the rock star he was on stage, all energy and confidence oozing off him, that huge, lovely smile on his face while he danced back and forth in front of the audience. His head was down, and I couldn't see his face, but everything in the way he held himself told me he was stressed—worn, even. He was sitting on the couch, his knees pressed to the edge of the coffee table, shoulders hunched over a notebook. He had a guitar squashed into his lap, one hand resting on the strings, the other holding a pen, and he was folded over the instrument like he was trying to make it part of him. His shoulders twitched, rolling inward, a protective gesture. He rocked his head from side to side, the pen tapping away at the paper. Then he dropped the pen and sat back. He smoothed his fingers over the guitar strings, but he did it so gently that no sound came out. His hand tensed, and he lifted it away from the guitar and made a fist, flexing his fingers, then shook it out. He closed his eyes, squeezing them shut, his other hand tight enough around the guitar's neck that his knuckles were going white.

I took another step into the room. I didn't really mean to, didn't even think about it. My fingers itched for a pencil and a scrap of paper. I wanted to draw him like this, wanted to compare the clean, sharp lines of those other sketches I had of him to this version, the curves I'd make of his spine, his hands, his shoulders, the roundness of his thoughts, as if I could see them circling in the shape of his body. But even more than that, I wanted to sit next to him and protect him from whatever it was that was wearing him down. There was something about him that seemed so fragile right then, so vulnerable, and so obvious that I wondered how I'd never seen it before. I wanted to offer myself up to it, spare him. Which was ridiculous. This was Bellamy. He certainly didn't need me to protect him.

My foot scraped over the carpet, and he jerked his head up. He was pale, his cheekbones shiny and sharp under his skin. His eyes were red, like he hadn't slept or he'd been rubbing at them. For a second, he just stared at me, his expression almost confused. It was like he couldn't tell if he wanted to ask me to come in or tell me to leave. I hadn't thought I'd want to stay, but when he met my gaze, backing up and leaving was the last thing I wanted to do. But he didn't ask me to. He grinned, and it was paper-thin, but it made his eyes sparkle a bit in that rock star way I knew. The hand that held the pen made a small gesture, a "come here" twist of his wrist. I stepped forward and sat down on the couch kitty-corner to his, almost next to him, but not quite.

I didn't have my sketchpad, and I regretted it, but I couldn't go back and get it now. I had my book, though, and opened it to my bookmark, holding it in my lap like I was planning to read it. I could still feel Bellamy's eyes on me. I glanced up, raising my eyebrows at him.

"Is it okay?" I waved my hand at the room. He'd offered, and I wanted the space from everyone else. But I'd still barged in. I didn't want to bother him.

His smile got wider somehow, the corners of his mouth lifting, and became more real at the same time. "Yeah. Stay."

I closed the book. "Are you . . . writing?" I flicked my fingers at the guitar, and his hands pressed against it. His body bent, curving around it the tiniest bit more.

He nodded. "Trying."

"Doesn't Tuck write with you?" Tuck was the lead guitarist, after all.

"Sometimes. Not the lyrics. I do those alone."

I knew that. I glanced down at the paper in front of him, covered in words and notes and crossed-out sections, some so black with ink they still looked wet. It was bizarre, to see it and put it together with the idea that he was writing lyrics, like the lyrics I'd been singing along to for years. Words I'd loved, that had made me feel good and sad and not alone, and had, sometimes, shifted the way I saw the world.

It was as if, by sitting here next to him and knowing he was working, he had pulled back the curtain for me. It felt personal, even though it was such a small thing. A magic trick revealed.

Bellamy sighed and sat back, flopping into the couch. He moved the guitar aside, setting it on the cushion beside him. One hand stayed wrapped around the neck. "What about you?"

I smoothed my thumb over the slick paper of the book cover. "I wanted a second to myself, actually."

Bellamy blinked at me. "I can go."

"No," I said quickly. I shook my head. "No. I could have gone to my bunk." I sounded tired to my own ears. I wished, not for the first time, that I could leave Eric behind. It was cruel of me, and guilt welled up in me whenever I wanted that, but I wished I could forget. I wished he couldn't hurt me anymore. That he would disappear from my mind and I wouldn't keep feeling this, over and over again.

"Are you okay?" he asked, his voice lower, gentler. He tipped his head forward, like he was studying me. I nodded.

Bellamy stared at me, trying to read something off my face, maybe. I knew he was probably waiting for me to say something else, to explain, but I couldn't. I didn't want to say it all again, right after I'd finished telling Ava. It was more than enough for one day. I wondered if coming into the room had been a mistake. It'd put us both on the spot, when we were still dancing around each other.

I was about to stand up and go when Bellamy leaned forward. "Well." He tapped his fingers down on the notebook page in front of him and ran them over the strings of words there. "If you wanted to stay here . . . I wouldn't mind." He glanced up at me through his bangs. He was grinning, sly and a little bit flirty. He still looked stressed, but it was somewhat less now.

I let out a short laugh. "No?"

He smiled back, his lips quirked to the side. "Yup. Imagine that—me, willing to share this teeny tiny room with you. I think I can just about manage."

I didn't say that my thoughts had actually been revolving around that exact question—if there was enough space for me, here, beside him. Not because the room was small, but because it felt small, and I was always afraid I was intruding on things and not noticing. I didn't have to say it, though. He was still grinning at me, like he knew exactly what I was thinking, and a blush was rising on my cheeks to prove he was right.

"We can distract each other," he added, and he didn't sound quite so much like he was teasing me anymore.

"Yeah?" I looked down to where his hand was still resting on the paper. His fingers had spread, almost like he wanted to cover it, block it from sight. "You want to be distracted too?"

He swallowed and nodded, and the grin slipped away. "Sometimes it's so easy, you know? Sometimes I just sit down and it happens and it's awesome. And sometimes . . . Sometimes I can't make myself focus on it. Like there's so much to pick through, I don't know where to start, what to hold on to. Like my mind doesn't even want to see it." He shook his head, as if he was trying to clear it. "And then that's all I can think about." His shoulders tensed, rising so they were almost hunched. "That I can't do it. That I'm getting everything wrong. And it makes everything worse."

He pressed his lips together, maybe trying his best to stop any more words from tumbling out. A pale-pink blush crept over his cheeks. He glanced up, and there was a question in his eyes. An uncertainty, like he was fragile or nervous.

"Bellamy. Are *you* okay?" I didn't know why I thought I should ask. He was fine. He was on tour with his band doing the things most people only dreamed about. Only he didn't quite look fine. He didn't look as happy as the rest of the band. Not happy like I'd seen him during a show, content and sure, like he was right where he belonged. Now he only looked hollowed out.

He nodded. "It's not important."

That wasn't quite the same as *It's nothing* or *I'm okay*, though.

I wanted to ask. I wanted to push it, because maybe there was something going on that was worrying him. Something with the band or the tour or even something back home. And if I could help . . .

But when it came down to it, Bellamy and I didn't actually know each other that well. And if he needed help or he needed someone to turn to, he'd go to his friends. He didn't need me.

He was still running the pen over his notebook, like if he stared at the words enough, they'd start to make sense to him. He had his knees pressed so hard to the coffee table that I could see where the table had started to slide across the carpet. He probably really had wanted to be alone, despite what he'd said. He probably hadn't wanted anyone to see him while he was in this . . . space. This thing that made him vulnerable and unsure.

But I did want to be distracted. I wanted to let him try. If he wanted the same, that was fine with me. "How? How do we distract each other?"

He considered, then raised his eyebrows at me. It surprised a smile out of me.

"Well," he said slowly, drawing out the word. He tilted his head to the side, considering. "You could talk to me. We seem to be pretty good at that." His mouth curled up at the corners, and he widened his eyes dramatically.

I huffed out a laugh, embarrassed. "Are you fucking with me?"

He pressed his lips together, trying not to laugh himself. "Yes, Micah. God, you're so cute." Which was funny, coming from him, since I was bigger than him, and I didn't think anyone had ever actually thought of me as cute before. But it made me blush too. "Get your sketchbook. Show me the drawings you won't let Tuck put up on the wall." He hesitated, and his eyes went dark and serious. "If you want to. You don't have to."

As if I was going to say no when he asked me like that—as a demand and not really a question, until he realized what he was doing. As if I'd say no to anything he wanted from me. Not that the idea of showing him my stuff didn't make me nervous. It was, honestly, terrifying. He was such an amazing artist, this perfect person, and I was only . . . me. A washed-up drummer with no aim and nothing going for me, clutching a sketchpad and pretending I had half a clue when it came to drawing, or anything else. But sketches were all they were, and it wasn't like he hadn't already seen what I could do. The stuff left in the book was mostly practice anyway. If he didn't like it, it wouldn't hurt too badly.

I went to my bunk and got the pad, and when I came back, he'd made room for me beside him on the couch. He patted the cushion in invitation, and I sat, keeping some distance between us. He closed it, though, snugging himself up beside me, the movement natural and totally unselfconscious. I tried to relax into the feeling of his shoulder against mine, his hip bumped up against me, his foot just touching my ankle, instead of tensing up and pulling away. It wasn't like I didn't want to be next to him like this. I just didn't want to want it so much. And I wanted it to be as special for him as it was for me, and it probably wasn't.

We went through the book, a picture at a time. Whenever I tried to skip ahead, pass over the drawings that were more experiments in light or form than anything else, he stopped me, a hand on my wrist or my knee, asking me to go back. He studied each one, and he seemed to be delighted by them. I'd have thought he was faking it, trying to make me feel good, but the way he stared at each sketch made me think he really did like them. It was a surprise to me, and maybe to him too. When he glanced up at me, I thought he looked at me differently. Like maybe he was really seeing me, as a person, as an individual, for the first time. And he thought whatever he saw was okay.

When we'd gotten all the way through, he closed the back cover, careful not to catch any of the pages in the spiral spine, and turned to me.

"Micah."

"Yeah."

"Are you having a good time?"

I turned to see him. He was so close I had to lean back to do it. "What do you mean?"

"Here. On tour, with us."

I shrugged. I hadn't really stopped to think about it much. It was a job. It was an escape, a way out of a circular pattern of thoughts and loss that probably would have drowned me, if I'd given them the chance. It was something for me to focus on.

"Yeah," I said after a second. I thought about watching Escaping Indigo every night, how that was something I'd never expected to be able to do, and something I loved. I thought about walking through the park with them, watching Bellamy let loose, hearing his laugh. How the band and Lissa and Quinn had taken me along with them and acted like I was part of them, like I had a place with them. Like I belonged. I hadn't expected that, either, had never expected that.

It had filled something inside me, something that I hadn't even really known was empty. "Why?"

"I just . . ." He rocked his head back and forth. "Sometimes you seem like you're getting lost in something that isn't us."

I swallowed. I didn't know what to say to that. Anything I did would sound melodramatic, or not dramatic enough. And I didn't want to think about it. Think about what I must be remembering, when Bellamy saw me that way. This was exactly what I hadn't wanted to get into with anyone.

"Sometimes you're like that too," I said instead, tossing it back to him. "Like you're . . . hiding something." That was what it was, I realized. He looked like he was hiding something. And I wanted to know what it was. But I didn't want to talk about my stuff. I could understand if he didn't want to talk about his.

Bellamy sighed, sounding almost content, and waved his hand lazily in front of him, pushing the whole conversation away.

We were quiet for a minute, and then Bellamy shifted, a tiny bit. I lifted my arm, and he ducked under it so I could put it around him. I stiffened when I realized what I'd done, but he seemed comfortable. It was a reflex movement, a position I'd sat in with Eric a thousand times, but it was just as natural with Bellamy. Like he fit beside me, and I fit around him.

I'd never been this nervous with Eric, though. He had never made me shiver and burn all at once.

"Is that the only tattoo you have?" he asked, breaking the slight tension.

"No. I have a couple others." My voice was a little breathy, but either he didn't notice, or didn't say anything.

"Where?"

I pulled my left foot up so I could roll up my jeans and show him the curl of words, a line from a book, around my ankle.

He nodded. "Oh, yeah, I've seen that one."

I moved slightly away and twisted so he could see the goldfish on the lower right side of my back. It was sentimental—a pretty thing that reminded me of the good parts of my childhood. I'd gotten teased about it some after I'd had it done. It had stung, being told that it was too pretty or too girly, but I hadn't cared that much, because I loved it. Bellamy didn't say anything, though. Just smiled.

Then I reached around and tapped the shoulder he'd been leaning on. He glanced up at me, and I nodded. His fingers reached for my collar.

"It's on the shoulder blade," I told him. "Near the top." My breath came quick, and my voice sounded ragged, even though I tried not to let it be. I'd shown people the tattoo before. I'd even explained it. But not often. And never without hurting inside.

He pulled back the fabric of my shirt, and I tipped forward so the light would hit my skin. I felt the brush of his fingers over the black ink. He lingered for a second, like he was staring at it. Then he let me go, and I sat back. I tugged roughly at the collar of my T-shirt to get it to sit right.

"Whose initial?" he asked. I could still feel the ghost of his fingers on me. He'd traced all the curves and lifts of the stylized E, and I thought I could feel the shape of it on me, outlined with his touch.

I looked at him. I could see the dark circles under his eyes, the tension around them.

I wasn't going to get out of this. But maybe . . . maybe that was okay, here, with him, in this quiet space.

I hesitated, then held out my arm, and he moved back into his spot against me, his breath warm against my neck. "A friend," I told him. Not a boyfriend—Eric and I had never been like that for each other, had never wanted to be. But not *just* a friend, either. A brother. I almost wanted to clarify, but maybe I didn't need to, not with Bellamy. Not with the way he loved his own friends. I wasn't sure why I could talk about Eric again, here, now, at all, when the same conversation had worn me so thin before. Maybe it was because it was only me and Bellamy in a cocoon the little room made around us, and I felt safe with him. Maybe it was because he'd asked so simply. "My best friend. He died."

His whole body went still, as if the words had frozen him, and his eyes went wide. I braced myself for whatever he was about to say. But he didn't say anything. He didn't question it, didn't ask how good a friend had to be before you tattooed him on yourself, how much you had to miss someone to do that. He didn't ask me anything else about

Eric at all, and I was glad. I didn't want to be sad, and I didn't want to go over it all again if I didn't have to. "It's pretty," was all he said, at last.

"Thanks."

"Do you want more? Tattoos?"

I nodded, and my cheek brushed his hair. His shoulder was warm under my hand. My fingers cramped with the desire to touch him, just a little, to have it be easy and right. I reached up and brushed his bangs back, tentative, and he tilted his head a bit, to give me better access. I stroked through his hair again. It was cool and soft between my fingers, and a bit tangled. "Someday. When I have money to spend." I wanted to be able to make enough that I could write and draw the things I thought were important into my skin. I wanted to be able to mark myself, claim myself for myself through the things I loved, the things that reminded me who I was.

"Was the Escaping Indigo one your first?"

I nodded again.

"Why?"

I shrugged my free shoulder. "It meant something to me, Bellamy." I didn't know how to explain it. How I'd loved getting it, how momentous it had been, to mark myself like that. How whenever I'd run my fingers over it afterward, I'd felt like maybe I wasn't alone, that there was something out there, the music, the band, that connected me to something else. That let me be myself. That reminded me that I could be strong. Even if that band never knew I existed. I would always have that connection. It would still be real. "It just meant something."

Bellamy's knee nudged mine. "Did I? Mean something?"

I didn't know how to answer him. His lyrics had meant something to me. They had meant a lot. So had the music behind them, the sounds of his guitar, the way his voice always captured me whenever I heard it. I'd always believed that those songs must have come straight from his heart, from his soul, because there was no way someone could write things like that and not mean them, not feel them, at least on some level. But some of those songs had been written almost a decade ago, maybe longer, and I didn't know how much of the Bellamy from those songs was in the Bellamy I was holding against me. The Bellamy who I'd been nervous with, was still nervous with, who had been sweet and distracted me when I was hurting, who was still gorgeous and captivating on stage, even when I was standing on the other side.

I still had my hand in his hair, those too long, cinnamon strands tangling around my fingers. I'd cut my own dark-brown hair short after Eric died, some nod to grief, a way to say I was devastated without saying it out loud. It was getting almost as long as Bellamy's now, though.

"Yeah," I told Bellamy. "You did."

He sighed, and I thought maybe he got even heavier. He wasn't exactly a small guy—lean, yes, but all of it wiry muscle, and I could feel each of his bones, all his sharp and heavy places, sinking against me. It wasn't uncomfortable, though. I liked the weight of him.

"Bellamy. Are you all right?"

He didn't move, but his body went a little tighter. His breathing quickened, until it was almost sharp. "Yup," he said after a second, and he shifted, almost shuddered, like he was trying to shake something off. He took a gulp of air, and another, and then he settled back against me.

I took a breath. It wasn't any of my business whether he was all right or not. But I'd never seen him like this before, never expected to. So quiet and withdrawn into his own mind. Maybe if I hadn't seen him struggling to write, fighting with himself, or if I hadn't caught him by himself in those still moments when he was smoking alone, I wouldn't have thought anything of it. But I had, and now I was. "Are you sure?"

He turned to me, his face tilting up, and I thought he'd say something, reassure me or brush me off or maybe both. But instead he hesitated, as if he was taking another deep breath or making a choice, and then he leaned in and pressed his lips against mine.

I was so startled, it was so unexpected, that for a second, I didn't kiss back. My body figured out what was happening before my brain did, and I launched myself at him, awkward and not subtle at all. My hands were in his hair, his lips were warm against mine, his arms were around my waist, and for a minute or two, it was perfect. Insanely perfect, like nothing I'd ever imagined, because I'd never imagined this happening with Bellamy. Gorgeous, wonderful Bellamy, who I'd spent so much time idolizing.

Then he was pushing me away, gentle, just enough that we could get some air.

"That's one way to be distracted," I mumbled.

"Sorry." His voice was low and raw. "Sorry. Shouldn't have."

"Why not?" I didn't even think about not asking. The words just tumbled out.

He was stroking a hand down my side like I was a cat. I wasn't sure he even knew he was doing it. "Bad idea. I've already scared off one roadie."

That hurt. It hurt enough that I wanted to pull back, but there was nowhere to go. The arm of the couch was against my back, and Bellamy was in front of me. "It was different, though, right?" I sounded so pathetically hopeful. I wanted to take it back as soon as I said it.

He shrugged and smiled, but it wasn't happy at all. "Sort of. I can't . . . I don't think it's a good idea. It's . . . I'm not good at this kind of thing."

I seriously doubted that. I couldn't imagine Bellamy not being good at anything. But I could see why he wouldn't want to get involved with a roadie again. Who knew if I'd even be here for long, after the tour?

I nodded, embarrassed and flushed and confused, and stood up. I wanted to escape, get back to my bunk, where I should have gone to begin with. But Bellamy caught my wrist.

"Micah. Don't . . . I'm sorry. Don't be angry with me."

I shook my head and plastered a smile on, even though I *was* angry. I just wasn't sure if I was angry at Bellamy or myself.

"It just . . . When it goes wrong, it hurts too much, you know?" He glanced down, and I might have thought he was putting on an act. But his fingers tightened around my wrist, like a spasm he couldn't control, and I believed him. "We're all crammed so close here. And I . . . I don't handle things well when they go wrong. I can't be messed up again. I can't let the band down. It's not only me. It's everyone, and I don't want to mess anything up."

I took a breath. I didn't understand what he was trying to say. Even if things didn't work between us, I couldn't see it pulling the whole band apart. That didn't make any sense. "You won't."

He looked up at me. His expression was perfectly flat. "You don't know me. You don't know what I'm like."

"Because you don't let me see." I didn't know where I was getting the courage to be so bold. Maybe it was his hand on me. The fact that he wasn't letting go.

He squinted at me. "You're right. We've all got secrets, don't we?"

I nodded. I saw his shadows, the things that lurked behind his eyes. I didn't know what they were, and he didn't seem to want to tell me. But they were there.

He nodded back and dropped my hand, and I bent to scoop my sketchbook off the table.

"I am sorry, Micah."

I shrugged, and it was easier this time. "I'm not angry." And I wasn't.

chapter five

after that night's show, we did laundry. Laundry had never been something I'd given much more than a passing thought to, if I even remembered to do it at all. But I'd never fully appreciated the ability to wash anything, the warm comfort of a clean T-shirt and jeans, anytime I wanted, until I didn't have the option anymore. Especially when I'd only brought a duffel bag's worth of clothes, and most nights I was sweating my ass off while I worked.

It seemed so simple, but it could be tricky to find time to do it on the road. We had a tiny portable thing that could wash a change of clothes, but it was never enough for all of us. But sometimes the venues had full-sized washers and dryers we could use. We tried to time it right, so we weren't all doing laundry at the same time, but this time, a combination of a venue with no washer and our first stretch of time on the road, and we were all arguing over who got to use the machines first. We let them run through the show—no one could hear a washer running over music and a thousand-plus screaming people—but I ended up getting stuck with the last load in, and I had to go back for it after Quinn and I had finished clearing the stage.

I headed through the stage door, wanting to grab my laundry out of the dryer and hightail it to my bunk. But I could hear people talking in the tiny laundry room, and I stopped. I didn't mean to eavesdrop, exactly. I didn't want to intrude on a conversation, though, and then I was listening in.

"Give it a rest. We don't have to start writing anything until we get home." That was Tuck's voice.

When Bellamy spoke, I could almost hear the shrug in his voice. "I know. I just . . . You know how I get. I think it'll be better if we start working on it now." He was probably trying to sound casual, but the tension in his voice was obvious. And if I could hear it, Tuck definitely could.

Tuck lowered his own voice. I could picture him leaning in to talk to Bellamy. "It's not going to do you or any of us any good if you force it when you're not feeling it, though. And you're not feeling it. I know you want to jump right into it, but . . . give yourself a break. Let this tour be easy for you. Don't let it be like last time."

There was a thump, and then Bellamy spoke again, his words harder and louder than before. "I know that, okay? But . . . telling me to stop isn't helping. Thinking you know what's going on in my head isn't helping, Tuck. It isn't. Leave me alone."

There were maybe five seconds of complete silence, but it felt so much longer than that. Then Tuck came out of the room, walking fast. He almost stopped when he saw me, and I started to hold up my hands, to apologize, anything, but he shook his head and brushed past me.

I waited a minute, not quite sure what to do. I wanted to turn around and go, pretend that I hadn't been here at all. But I still had to get my laundry. They'd be wanting to lock the venue up soon, and I had to be out of there with my clothes before then.

When I poked my head around the door, Bellamy was standing over my laundry basket, folding a towel. His back was to me, and I could see the tightness in his shoulders, the way he was hunching them. He dropped the towel, reached down for it, and it slipped through his fingers a second time before he got a grip on it again. He yanked it up, almost angrily, but there was a fragility to his movements, to the way he held himself, that made me think he was only just holding himself together. He shook the towel out with a snap and folded it neatly, his hand smoothing over the cotton a few times, as if he was soothing himself with the tidiness of it.

"Is that my stuff?" I asked.

He flinched, hard, and I felt bad. When he turned to look at me, I thought he might actually be blushing, but the flickering light made it too hard to see. He nodded and dropped the towel on a short stack of other towels in the basket.

"I knew it was going to take you a while to load all the gear, so . . . Sorry for touching your stuff. But I figured you'd be tired. I didn't touch your boxers. Just left them in the bottom."

I should probably be weirded out by it, but I wasn't. I'd shove Quinn's and Bellamy's and even Ava's laundry in and out of dryers, simply because I was the guy who was there to do it. And Bellamy had folded everything for me, even my jeans.

I also wanted to laugh at the image in front of me, of a man who'd been on stage an hour before, sweaty and breathtaking and making people fall in love with him and his music, folding my laundry like it was an important task.

"Thank you."

He nodded and flopped down on the rickety plastic chair someone had pulled up to an old card table. "Did you see Tuck?"

I hesitated, then nodded.

Bellamy tipped his head back and sighed. "I've got to go apologize to him."

"Okay." I went over and hoisted up my full laundry basket. I could feel the warmth of the clean clothes, smell the fabric sheet scent of them. There was something strangely comforting about that, and I just wanted to grab a blanket, put on my newly clean pajamas, and climb into bed. I was willing to bet that Bellamy was as tired as I was, more so because he'd been the one up on stage, giving pieces of himself away. "Go find him. And then I'll meet you back at the bus, all right?"

He blinked up at me. He didn't smile, and I wondered how much the argument with Tuck had upset him. It had only been small, but I hadn't ever heard them arguing about anything before. He nodded at me. "Okay. Did you hear . . .?"

I rolled my shoulders. I didn't want to admit I'd been listening, but I wasn't going to lie about it. "Only a little."

"Was I too harsh?" he asked softly.

I shook my head, shifted the basket against my hip. "No." I didn't really know what they'd been talking about, but I could guess some of it. "But I think he thought he was protecting you."

He pressed his lips together. "That's not his job."

"So tell him that." I took a deep breath. I wasn't anyone who could tell someone else what to do with a relationship. I had never been very good at that, and Eric had only stuck around with me because he knew how awkward I could be. But I knew, too, that Tuck and Bellamy were friends, close friends, and this was probably something that was bothering them both. "And you can apologize to him too. If you want."

He nodded again and stood up. "I do want to." He reached out as he walked past and ran his fingertips over my wrist. "Thank you."

I watched him go, then checked to make sure no stray laundry had been left by anyone. I met up with the security guard and told him we'd cleared out, and then I went to the bus.

It was dark, and everyone, as far as I could tell, had gone to bed. There was always a chance someone was working off insomnia in the back room, but I didn't hear any sound coming from there. I walked to the bunks and the little cubbies beside them, where we kept our stuff. The promise of a cozy bed was the only thing keeping me on my feet at this point, and I shoved my stuff in without really paying attention—but with enough care to make sure Bellamy's folding job didn't go to waste. I went to the miniscule bathroom and changed into pajamas, and came back ready to hop right into my bunk.

Except when I got there, someone was already there, tucked into the corner. My heart skipped, even while I told myself it was only Bellamy, and I had to stop and put a hand to my chest.

"Goddamn you. You scared me."

"Sorry." He leaned forward so I could see his face. "I thought you saw me before."

I shook my head. I hadn't even while I'd been putting my stuff away.

"Jesus, Bellamy." My heart rate was going back to normal, but I could still feel it skipping around. "What are you doing up there?" I lowered my voice. "Did you find Tuck?"

He nodded. "Yeah. Thank you."

He didn't say whether everything was resolved, and I didn't ask. He didn't look like he was planning on going anywhere, either. I waited, not sure what I should do, but he didn't move, so I hoisted myself up next to him. He leaned farther back into the corner, so

I pulled the curtain shut behind me. I wanted to talk to him, I just didn't want to wake everyone else up. A curtain wasn't going to block all sound, but it was better than nothing, and it made the little bunk a bit more of a private place.

"Bellamy. You okay?"

"Huh?" He picked his head up from where it had been sliding into my pillows. He was wearing a T-shirt and boxers, like he'd been ready to get into his own bed. He'd just gotten into mine instead. "Yup. Can I stay here tonight?"

"What?" I tried not to sound panicked, but . . . I was sort of panicked. This was a seduction technique I hadn't encountered before. Although I thought Bellamy was too worn out for seduction of any kind.

"I just . . . I want to stay here." The words were simple, but there was a tiny tremor in his voice, as if he was on the edge of something. I wondered, if I was touching him, if I'd feel that tremor in his body, if he'd shiver against me. His eyes were too wide, bright even in the dark, and he sounded so earnest and hopeful that I would let him stay. I didn't know why he wanted someone next to him. I didn't know why he'd picked me. But I wanted to do that for him.

I eyed the tiny bunk. We were already squished in. But he looked warm and cozy, and as strange as this all was, I didn't want to make him go. If I was being honest with myself, I wanted to continue what had happened between us the night before. Or, at least, I didn't want to push away the possibility of that someday continuing. I wanted to make him comfortable. I wanted to give him whatever he needed.

I prodded his legs until he moved over, enough that I could stretch out behind him and wrap an arm around his waist. I was right. There was a tension in his body, a tremble under the skin, almost. As if he was about to start shaking. He didn't, though. But it took a long time for the tension to bleed out of him.

Our heads were close together on the pillow, his hair soft against my face, hips nestled right into mine. His back expanded against my chest when he breathed. It was startlingly intimate.

"All right?"

He nodded, a tiny movement. His hand came up, and he caught my fingers. "Thanks."

I resisted the urge to kiss the back of his neck, but it was hard. "Are you okay, Bellamy?" I asked again, gentler this time. I wanted him to know I really wanted an answer. "You can tell me things, you know. I know I'm . . . just the roadie, and you're . . . you, but you can tell me. I can listen."

His fingers tightened. "You're not just the roadie, Micah. Don't think that, okay? I'm sorry if I made you feel like that." He sighed, and seemed to sink deeper into the pillow. "Tuck told me I should stop pushing people away."

"Oh."

"He meant it in a nice way." His voice was getting lower, going breathy with sleep.

"I'm sure he did." I was. I hadn't spent too much time with Tuck, but everything about him told me he was a good guy. I didn't think Ava or Bellamy or even Quinn would have been touring with him if he wasn't.

"You're one of those people I should stop pushing away."

"I . . ."

"I liked kissing you."

I felt like the ground had dropped out from under me. "I liked it too."

"Good." I couldn't see his face, but I thought his eyes were probably closed. He sounded like he was drifting off. I wondered if in the morning he'd remember talking about this. It made me want to be brave, take the chance I had.

"Are you going to do it again?"

"Maybe." He sounded so honest, like he was really thinking about it, that I had to stifle a laugh. "Not right now, though."

I did kiss his neck then, the delicate patch of skin just below his hair. "No. Now we're going to sleep."

We did sleep, wrapped around each other like that. In the morning, Bellamy was already gone. I didn't know how he'd gotten out of the bunk without waking me, but he had. He flashed me a shy smile when I finally saw him, but he didn't say anything about the night before, and I was too nervous to ask. But I could still feel the shape of him in my arms, and I hoped that last night had meant something to him.

chapter six

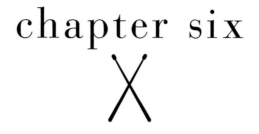

the next night, we were in Philadelphia, and after the concert almost everyone went out for coffee and desserts, and maybe to see if they could find something fun to do. I begged off and went back to the bus by myself, and found Bellamy there.

He was pacing back and forth, his hands jammed in the back pockets of his jeans, his head down. He must not have heard me come in, and his back was to me as he walked the length of the front room of the bus. For a second I thought maybe something was really wrong, because he looked so upset, but I couldn't pinpoint why I thought that. He wasn't acting strangely. He was just . . . moving. Like he didn't want to stop. Like he was trying to bleed off some energy, even though, not more than an hour ago, he'd exhausted himself on stage, putting everything he had into his performance. I knew he had. I'd seen it.

He paused and pulled his hands out of his pockets, and shook them, as if he were shaking water off his fingertips.

When he pivoted to start up his pacing again, he saw me. It was too late to pretend I hadn't seen his . . . meltdown or whatever it was. He could see it on my face, I was pretty sure. I straightened my shoulders, ready to say . . . something. The expression on his face made me think he'd do the same, try to brush this off. But then his shoulders collapsed inward and he turned and slumped on the couch, his back curled, his hands in his lap. It was as if someone had taken all the stuffing out of him.

I took another step into the room. "Hey." I was surprised to see him here at all. I hadn't seen him go out with the others, but he'd disappeared right after the band got off the stage, and he hadn't come back.

He smiled at me, a bit wobbly, the expression knowing, as if we were sharing a secret and we were both well aware of it. "Hey." He let his head tilt back.

"You okay?" I tried to add this picture of him up with the ones I had of him behind the mic, or when he'd been standing on the top of that slide in the park. I couldn't quite do it. He looked more as he had the other day, when I'd found him trying to write lyrics. Like he was sinking into his own world and blocking everyone else out. Like there was something inside him trying to escape.

"Uh-huh." He blinked at me. "Just tired. You didn't go out with everyone else?"

I shook my head and made myself move. I walked past him, over to the fridge, and bent down in front of it. "No. I've got Chinese leftovers. Nothing better." I didn't mention that I was tired too, after the show tonight and our evening the night before, and that was the real reason I hadn't gone with everyone else. Too little sleep, too many new emotions to feel. I wanted a break from it, and from what I'd seen, he could use one too. I *did* want to talk to him about the night before, but I thought maybe we were both too worn out for it right now, and I didn't know where to start.

He laughed softly. "Unless someone ate them." His voice was slightly unsteady, but if I hadn't seen him a few minutes before, I didn't think I'd have even considered that everything wasn't fine.

I pulled open the fridge door. "Heads will roll. You can't eat someone else's leftovers."

He made a humming noise. "I completely agree."

No one had stolen my leftovers. I pulled them out, stuffed them in the microwave, and turned back to him while the microwave did its thing.

I braced my hands against the short counter and studied him. He had his eyes closed, his head resting against the couch. I'd never have known, if I'd been in the audience tonight, that maybe he wasn't feeling his best. He'd been as amazing as ever. Tonight, he'd actually jumped into the crowd, aiming for a group of big guys in the front who had caught his slender body easily. He'd let the fans toss him back and forth, the mic still clutched in his hands, the lyrics spilling out of him in breathless gasps. I'd watched him from my place on the stage, feeding the cord to him so he didn't get tangled or have to let go of the mic. He'd stared up at the ceiling, but I hadn't thought he'd really seen it. His expression had been so far away, his eyes wide and his gaze distant. When the fans had dumped him back on the other side of the fence, he'd shaken himself, as if he was coming down from something huge, and he had to shake whatever it was off. I'd offered my hand to pull him back on the stage, and he'd gazed through me like I wasn't even there. He'd never stopped singing, though, never missed a note. He'd given all of himself to those people. I didn't know how he did it, night after night. I couldn't imagine giving that much of myself away.

"You looking for some space?" I asked. It had become almost a code between us, something safe to ask. I tried to be casual about it, but I wasn't really sure which way I wanted him to answer.

He met my eyes and shook his head.

"Okay," I said. The microwave dinged, and I turned back around.

I moved around the tiny kitchen for a minute, grabbing utensils and napkins. I hesitated, then went and sat next to Bellamy. I handed him a fork.

"What's this?"

"A fork." I opened the Styrofoam box and stared into it, carefully not catching his eye. "This lo mein is amazing. And you haven't eaten all day."

He twirled the fork in his fingers. "And how do you know that? You been watching me?"

I lowered my own fork and twisted to face him. He rolled his head on the back of the couch and stared at me. His lips curved into a slow, teasing grin. Most of his steadiness was back in place, and that confidence was like a weight, especially when held up against what I felt when I looked at him—that he was beautiful and bold and I was small and insignificant and unimportant.

"I haven't been watching you," I told him, my voice soft, the embarrassment obvious in it. I tried not to think about it, and glanced away so I couldn't read on his face what he was seeing in me. I really hadn't been keeping tabs on him. But I knew already that sometimes he got so wrapped up in the music, in the writing and the playing, in the new cities, that he forgot to eat. That sometimes Tuck had to make a sandwich for him and actually place it in his hand, to make sure he'd put it in his mouth. And I knew everyone had been distracted today, busy, and that even if he'd eaten lunch, he hadn't eaten since. I grabbed his arm and steadied the fork in his hand, pushing my embarrassment away, or at least to the back of my mind. "But I know you need to eat. So just . . . eat with me."

He looked down, that sly grin slipping off his face, showing the weariness underneath. But he stuck his fork into the food without any further argument.

We took turns scooping up the lo mein, trying to make the thick noodles twist around the tines of the forks. Chopsticks would have been better, but all I'd had were those disposable ones last night, and I'd tossed them. Bellamy laughed, a low huff of amusement, whenever my forkful slithered back to the container before I could get it to my mouth. I would have been self-conscious if he hadn't been so delightfully amused by it. I liked that I could make him happy, even for a second, even with something ridiculous. I liked being able to sit with him and pretend we were just two people, equals.

When he'd had enough, he set his fork in the top half of the container and slumped back against me, sitting almost the way he had the afternoon before. Like his head belonged at rest on my shoulder. He folded his hands in his lap, tucked his feet up under him, and I knew without turning to see that his eyes were closed. I forked up another bite, careful not to jab him with my elbow.

"I'm sorry about your friend," he said. The words were soft, but they still sent a nasty chill through me.

"What?" I froze with the fork halfway to my mouth.

"I'm sorry. I . . . I felt bad. I hinted at it to Ava, and she said you'd talked . . . I'm sorry I said anything to her, Micah. I didn't want to gossip. I just felt so bad."

I took the bite, then dropped my fork with Bellamy's. I closed the container and leaned over to set it on the end table beside us. I tried to decide if I was angry. I'd come on tour with Escaping Indigo to get away from this. But this, this lifestyle, this band . . . It was all so tied up in Eric. Maybe I'd actually been running toward something that would remind me of him.

"It's okay," I told Bellamy. This wasn't the conversation I'd wanted, tonight, but it looked like the one I was going to have. I took a deep breath. "I'm sorry your boyfriend was such a jerk." We were sitting so close again, and I could feel the heat of him, his tiny movements. Could feel the way he was almost leaning into me. I leaned into him instead, and he didn't move away. "You didn't get to say good-bye to him, right?" I wasn't sure why I was asking. Because I was thinking about Eric, maybe. Thinking about how weird it was to love someone and then have them simply be . . . gone.

Bellamy slumped. "Nope. We weren't really . . . We didn't do a lot of talking, at the end. We were . . . always fighting. Me trying to get a rise out of him. Start something. Don't think he wanted to talk to me much."

I shifted, so he could tuck in against me if he wanted to. I wasn't very subtle about it. But he went with it, pressing close. I tried to keep my breathing even, not let my nervousness show. "Why?"

His hand brushed mine. "I guess . . . it felt like we were still connected, when we fought. Like we were still doing something together. Like he still saw me."

I caught one of his fingers with my pinky. "Did you love him?"

He sighed. "Sometimes. Never in a way that worked."

"Not all roadies are complete jerks, you know."

He tightened his finger on mine. "I know."

He sounded so tired. I thought he might fall asleep, right there next to me on the couch. I wondered where that energy from before had gone, and then I wondered if it had ever really been there at all, or if what I'd seen had been something else.

"What did you do before you were our roadie, Micah?"

I took a slow breath. "Ava didn't tell you?"

He shook his head against my shoulder.

"I was a drummer. And," I added reluctantly, "a cashier at a grocery store."

"You like this better?"

"Than being a cashier?" I huffed out a dry laugh. "Yes."

"Not better than being a drummer, though."

I shook my head. "No one wants to work for someone else's band if they can be in their own." That wasn't exactly true. I was happier than I'd thought I would be, doing just that.

"So why aren't you? In your own band?"

I reached up and tapped my shoulder, where Eric's initial was. It felt like an excuse. It *was* an excuse. But it was all I wanted to explain, right then.

He watched my hand move, and when I dropped it back in my lap, he took it in his, twining us together this time, instead of simply letting our fingers bump.

"I like this," I said into the quiet. "It's what I wanted, and Quinn made it happen for me. For now it's . . . I like it. It's good."

Bellamy didn't say anything for a long moment, just sat next to me. It should have been boring to sit here, in the near dark, not talking, not doing anything. But it wasn't. It was comforting and nerve-racking at the same time. I wanted to bring up the kiss again. I wanted to know what had gone wrong there. But at the same time, I didn't want anything but to keep sitting here like this.

"I wanted to say good-bye," Bellamy said at last. "I missed him." His voice was so soft, like it might get lost in the dark around us. "I would have been good with . . . just a fucking note or something. Not even an apology. Just . . . an end." He turned to me. "You know?"

I nodded. I knew.

"Did you get a good-bye with the guy tattooed on your shoulder?"

"No." Eric had overdosed alone in his room. I'd seen him for band practice, and the next day, he'd been dead.

I turned, and he was watching me, his face so close. He held my eyes.

"Micah," he said, even though I was already looking right at him.

"Yeah."

"Why aren't you in a band? Really?" His voice had gone all easy and deep, and it made me want to answer him. But it was complicated and confusing, and I didn't know how to do it honestly.

I stared down at my hands, our fingers twisted together. "Eric died."

"I'm sorry," he said. "I'm so sorry. But . . ." I looked back up at him, and he was staring off into the dark of the bus. "But does that mean you can't be in a band with someone else? Ever?"

I shook my head. "No. It's . . ." I sighed. I never knew how to tell people what I felt about this. What I wanted. "It's gone. You know? All of it. Everything I wanted, I wanted with Eric. The place I belonged . . . was always with him. Because of him. Now he's gone, and I'm stuck with just half of everything, half of all the things we hoped for, and it's all useless."

"But . . ." he started, and I held up my free hand.

"He made me better." I caught Bellamy's eye, then ducked my head. "I'm a good drummer. I'm really . . . I was good at it." I glanced up to see Bellamy smiling, and I grinned too, embarrassed, acknowledging how ridiculous it felt to say that about myself. Then I looked down again, focused on our hands. "I wanted to be a musician. I wanted it to work, for us to be successful. I wanted that more than anything. But Eric made me want it more. He made me want to be a drummer more. He made me want all of it . . . more."

Bellamy tightened his fingers on mine, and shifted closer, enough that we were all lined up down one side. Like he was trying to give me something to lean on, something to hold me up.

"You have to be good," I continued. "But mostly, to make it work, you have to want it more than anything else. You have to breathe it and dream it when you sleep; you have to be immersed. You have to crave it, all of it. The making music and the playing and the concerts and the touring—all of it. You know that. You must know that." I turned to him. He was staring at me, his hair curling in his face, tangled and unruly from the way he'd toweled himself off after the show. I remembered who it was I was talking to—a rock star. And I was trying to tell him how hard it was to do this. I caught my breath, mortified.

He just nodded, though, and held my eyes. I had to look away. I wished we were sitting farther apart, so I didn't have to focus on the warmth coming off him, on how he always sat so close, on how much I wanted to kiss him again.

"I don't want it like that anymore," I said, my voice softer than before. "I'm lost without it. I don't know what the fuck to do with myself, honestly. But I don't want it enough anymore. After Eric . . . I just don't. And I think . . . I think I had my shot. Eric and me, we would have made it. He would have taken me there. But now . . . I don't think you get that lucky twice in a lifetime."

"Not if you think like that," he said, almost under his breath.

I raised my eyebrows at him. "Yeah, no. But that's how I want to think. Okay?"

He stared back at me, his eyes taking me in, a little wider than normal, maybe. Like he was surprised. Or like he was really seeing me for the first time, seeing something he hadn't expected. "Don't you miss it?"

I let out a small laugh. "Yeah. I miss it." I missed it like I was missing a limb. Like part of me had disintegrated and I could never find it again, could never really put myself back together. I wasn't sure how much of that, though, was me missing being in a band, and how much of it was me missing Eric, me missing the time we'd spent together, making music, creating songs, merging our ideas and our sounds. I didn't care. I figured the two would always go hand in hand, for the rest of my life, like they had while he'd been alive.

I had that weird calm going on that sometimes happened after a show—not right after, but after I'd had time to absorb the music and the noise and the lights and the riot of input. After the body had accepted what had been put into it. It didn't matter that I hadn't actually stood in the crowd. All that mattered was that I'd been in the heart of the music, surrounded by it, encased in it. And now Bellamy and I were sitting in the quiet, and the absence of all that sound sank into me and swallowed me as surely as the music had. Maybe more, because it was such an opposite to the sound that had been there before. It made me feel whole and lucky, complete and satisfied. It made me feel bold and strong, where any other time, I would have been shy. "I'm not the rock star you are, Bellamy. I'm not built for this like you, and Ava, and Tuck. Not anymore. Not without Eric."

He went so still. "I don't know if anyone's actually built for this, Micah."

It struck me, then, how odd it was to be having this conversation at all. To be sitting here with Bellamy, someone I had admired for so long from such a distance. To have him be real and human and fragile beside me. It was terrifying, and I kept wondering if I was having some hallucination, if I'd wake up and find that I had only imagined all of this. But I also liked Bellamy even better like this. I liked knowing he was a person, and not only the fantasy I'd created and held on to in my mind.

Didn't mean I wasn't nervous too, though. But it made me want to take risks and, maybe, be as vulnerable back.

"Bellamy," I said. He nodded against my shoulder. I could feel his breath on my neck, and I tried not to shiver. "What you said about your boyfriend . . . about being afraid of getting hurt . . . I wouldn't do that. I want you to know."

He laughed softly. "You can't really promise that."

I took a deep breath, and then had to take another to steady myself. "I could try."

His hand jumped in mine, but he didn't let go. "It's not about you trying, or anyone trying. It's that . . ." He drifted off, and for a long few minutes, he was silent. "Never mind." He didn't say it like he was trying to be coy. He said it like he'd had this conversation a hundred, a thousand times before, and he was done with it. "It's not important."

I twisted so I could see him. "If it's not important, then why did you stop kissing me the other day?"

He sucked his lower lip into his mouth, then let it go. "I don't know."

"Do you remember what you said to me, last night, in my bunk?" I was pressing him, and I knew it could all end up so backward. But I wanted . . . something. I wanted out of this weird impasse where I didn't know what was going on between us. I wanted to know if I should hope for anything. Or if I shouldn't.

He might have been smiling, but if he was, it was so small I almost couldn't see it. "What are you asking me, Micah?"

I swallowed. My throat was so dry. "I'm asking you to kiss me again. Not for anything more complicated than that. Just . . . kiss me."

For what felt like the longest minute ever, he didn't move. Then he leaned forward, slower this time, so I could see his face come closer, could see the honey-brown flecks in his eyes, could study all the ways the low light turned his hair gold and nutmeg. So I could see that he looked nervous and serious and determined. And then he kissed me. It was so sweet. Soft and gentle and persistent. He cupped his hand around the back of my head, and he was so tender and careful and demanding, all at once, that I thought this must be what want felt like. I felt immediately full of myself, thinking I could be someone Bellamy would want. But he kissed me like I was special, and I could taste it.

We kissed for a long time, and he didn't try for anything else. There was still a tiny space separating us on the couch. I wanted to bridge it, wanted to pull him into my lap, or suggest we see how well we'd fit into a bunk when we were pressed even closer together. But I was too nervous—asking to be kissed had taken up all of my bravery. And I didn't want to break the spell, whatever was happening between us. This, this alone, was enough.

In the end, it didn't matter. The door to the tour bus flung open, admitting loud voices and laughter. Bellamy and I broke apart, and it took me a second to come back to myself and realize the rest of the band had returned.

I turned to Bellamy and found him flushed, his lips slightly swollen. He was clenching his hands in his lap, and I realized I missed having them on me. He wasn't quite meeting my eye.

If the others knew something was up, they didn't say anything. Ava gave us a long stare, and I thought she raised her eyebrows at me. But Bellamy wasn't making any move to touch me or even look at me again, so I didn't, either. I just sat there, even more uncertain than before. Awkward. Feeling like I shouldn't have dared to kiss Bellamy to begin with.

Bellamy got up to go to bed before the rest of us. Making an escape, I thought, and I couldn't really blame him. I didn't feel real warm and fuzzy about it either, though. But when he walked past me, he brushed my hand with his, his fingers doing a slow, deliberate trail over my palm. And then I didn't know what to feel at all.

X

That night, when I curled up in my bunk, pressing myself tight to the wall, I let my fingers wander up to the *E* tattooed on my shoulder, and watched the glow from the streetlamp play along the edge of the curtain. I'd wanted the tattoo so that I'd never forget. It was stupid to think I would, but like keeping the set lists, there was an irrational fear there that I couldn't shake. And, sometimes, that fear felt so legitimate. I couldn't remember the exact depth of Eric's voice anymore. Couldn't remember what he'd smelled like. I couldn't remember how his hand had felt on my arm. I could still picture him, the manic smile he'd give me when we were on stage together, the way his piercings had caught the bright lights and thrown them like sparks back at me. The way his hair flopped over to the right side of his face. But the movement he'd made a thousand times a day to brush that hair back out of his eyes was fuzzy in my memory. I wasn't sure, anymore, if, when I pictured him hunched over a guitar, I was picturing it exactly *right*. I was afraid that someday I'd wake up and wouldn't remember what he'd looked like. Wouldn't remember how good it had been to have him beside me, to be able to rely on him, to love him.

So I'd gotten the tattoo out of that fear. But I'd put it on my shoulder blade because I couldn't bear to see it all the time.

Now I ran the pads of my fingers over it. I couldn't really feel it. There were a couple of places where the ink was still raised, thick under my skin. But I wouldn't have known what shape I was tracing if the image of the tattoo wasn't etched in my mind. I could picture it so perfectly, though. The black lines, the shadows around it, subtle. I'd told the artist I wanted an *E*, that was all, but he'd made it something beautiful that had become a part of me, that was lovely and very much mine, even when I didn't want to look at it.

But that's what it was—a part of me, a memory that I had, and not really part of Eric at all. When I ran my fingers over it, it forced me to remember, and sometimes I needed that. Needed to be reminded of what it was like to have him. But it wasn't like he was any closer to me. I never felt like he was here. Some people thought ghosts lingered, felt it, like there was some residual spirit or something, but Eric was just . . . gone. He wasn't watching over me or any of that other bullshit. He was gone.

I wanted Eric here, right now. I didn't want touching the tattoo and remembering to have to suffice. I wanted to ask Eric what he thought of Bellamy, wanted to ask him what he thought I should do. Eric hadn't been a people person, but he'd been damn good at reading things. It was why he'd been so great at the front of a stage. He'd known how to make people fall in love with him. He'd have known how to ask Bellamy what he was hiding. Eric would have known how to make Bellamy comfortable. Would have known how I should ask if Bellamy really wanted me.

But he wasn't here, and I couldn't talk to him about a single thing. Instead, I lay there and touched the tattoo, and wished things had turned out so differently.

chapter seven

X

two days later, we were in muggy but beautiful Atlanta, Georgia. I'd never been there before, either, hadn't been to most of the places we'd gone, and I tried to capture in my mind something specific about the city so I'd remember later. It was just . . . so green. So very city-like, with its concrete and huge, wide roads, but still so overwhelmingly green. I liked it here.

Escaping Indigo had an interview at a radio station and then a signing at a local music shop. After they'd gone, I met up with Quinn. He was peering into the back of the trailer and poking at equipment, getting ready to start hauling it out and setting it up.

"We got house help?" I tugged the bass drum, snug in its case, closer to me.

"Yup. I told them to wait, though. We've got lots of time. No sense in them standing around while we pull stuff out."

I found myself studying him while he shifted instruments and gear around. I realized that, since we'd started touring, Quinn and I hadn't spoken very much outside of our jobs. He was busy all the time, driving and running sound and making sure everything was going smoothly. Quinn wasn't the official manager of Escaping Indigo, but he did everything that a manager would, plus extra. The band was decently popular—popular enough to play theaters, not popular enough that they were getting mobbed in the street by fans—but they couldn't afford to hire too many extra people. The bus itself was a luxury. I was lucky Quinn had needed help, or I wouldn't be there. I thought he liked staying busy and taking care of everyone. Taking care of me. It took his mind off things. But Quinn was recovering, or not recovering, from losing Eric, the same way I was.

Quinn and I had never really been friends. We'd just been connected by the same person. When we'd lost him, I'd expected to lose Quinn too, even though I was still living above his mother's garage. We hadn't seemed to have anything between us anymore. But it turned out that we did—we had the hole Eric had left. There was almost no one else on the planet who could quite understand what it'd been like to lose Eric, to lose the person I'd considered a brother. It made me feel guilty for not paying more attention to Quinn now, while we were on the road. For getting so wrapped up in myself and Bellamy and not even thinking about what he was going through.

"How are you?" He glanced at me, and I wondered what expression I'd had, that he'd felt like he should ask. "Are you doing okay? Being on the road? After ... everything?"

I set down the cymbal bag I was holding. I wanted to nod, but I couldn't quite make myself do it. I did something that was halfway between a nod and a shrug.

He gestured me around the other side of the trailer, so we could lean our backs against it and look out, past the venue and the parking lot to the street beyond. He dug around in his pocket and came up with a pack of gum. He pulled out a piece and offered it to me. I took it with raised eyebrows.

"I'm trying to quit smoking," he said with an apologetic shrug.

I shrugged back. I thought chewing gum was a big waste of time and teeth, but I stuffed it in my mouth anyway. "Thanks."

"Yup." He turned to me. "Okay. Want to try answering that question again?"

I rolled my shoulders back and stared out at the road. It was empty, slick with heat in the midday sun. "I'm fine."

"How fine?" he asked, soft, serious, and I couldn't help but face him. "I know the last time you were on the road, it was with Eric. I know the music . . ." He trailed off and made a vague gesture with his hand. "I know."

I opened my mouth to repeat that I was fine, just fine, but he wasn't smiling, wasn't looking pitying, wasn't any of what I'd come to expect from people who knew I was grieving. He was just asking, just wanted to know. I thought about the hundred, thousand times a day when I did or saw or said something and wished Eric was beside me, the new things I felt every day that didn't quite feel real, because I couldn't tell him about them. I thought about how badly I just wanted to hear his voice, how I had that thought so often it was like a constant refrain running through the back of my mind. How every time I saw Escaping Indigo on stage, I wondered about what could have been. How far Eric would have gone. How many people would have fallen all over him to love him, like they did for Bellamy.

I thought, right then, that the phrase "misery loves company" was a completely bullshit one. I hoped Quinn wasn't feeling a fraction of what I was, because it was awful. I didn't wish this on anyone.

"I miss him," I blurted out. "I keep thinking he should be here, that this should be us, and it's not. And I can't call him, and I can't ask his opinion, and I *need* him. I don't know who I am without him." I sucked in a breath, nearly gasping, embarrassed and horrified by what I was saying, and weirdly relieved to have it out there. Although I wished it hadn't been Quinn that I'd spilled it all over.

But Quinn only nodded, and turned to face forward again. He reached out and wrapped his hand around my arm, holding me steady, connecting us with that little contact. Making it okay for me to have said all that, for us to stand here and accept that we were hurting. It wasn't the right time for us to be sad. It was, it seemed, never quite the right time. But sometimes it snuck up on me, and I supposed it did the same to Quinn.

"Bellamy isn't Eric," he said after we'd been quiet for a long minute.

It took me by surprise. "I know." It would have been hard to think they were anything alike. Bellamy was day to Eric's night.

Quinn shook his head. "I just . . . He doesn't need saving like Eric did."

My spine went stiff. "Eric didn't need saving." He'd needed direction. Help. He'd needed to realize that what he was doing was bound to kill him. But no one person had been going to save him, except himself.

Quinn sighed and ran his hand through his hair. I stared at him. He was such a fixture in my life, Eric's big brother, always there, that I'd stopped really noticing him a while ago. He was just Quinn. But now I took a second and really studied him. He looked . . . almost the same as he always had. His beard was scruffy, but it had always grown like that: a coarse stubble that he simply didn't bother to shave often enough. His dark hair brushed the top of his ears. He had gauges in his lobes. Eric had had the same gauges. On him, they'd been exotic and unusual and sexy. They'd accentuated the curve of his cheekbones. They made Quinn appear rough and wild. He was big where Eric had been small, his shoulders broad and built, the muscles in his body obvious. He was blunt and straightforward and logical, where Eric had been flighty and dreamy, thoughts flying in and out of his head so fast sometimes I hadn't been able to keep up with him. It had always amazed me that he and Quinn were brothers. But in the sun, Quinn's skin was the same color Eric's had been: tan and freckled. His mouth had the same shape. When he shoved his hair back, he did it the same way Eric had, the movement so eerily similar that whenever he did it, it made me look twice.

"Who are you trying to protect?" My voice was even, not quite angry. "Me or Bellamy?"

"Both of you. You." He gave a shrug that was uncomfortable and tight. "Eric did a good job of trying to rip you apart. I don't need Bellamy to finish the job."

I leaned back against the warm metal behind us. The sentiment was a kind one, but it didn't say much about my ability to make choices for myself.

"Why do you care?" I folded my arms over my chest, but it made me feel like a kid defying an adult, so I uncrossed them again.

Quinn's eyes went wide, and he glanced over at me and back down to the pavement, like he was working out something to say. But he didn't answer.

"I mean," I continued, "I'm not your responsibility. We weren't ever even friends." I wasn't trying to be cruel. But it was the truth. I lowered my voice. "I'm grateful for what you've done for me, Quinn, getting me this job and everything. But I don't . . ." I shook my head. "I don't get why you're worried about me."

"Eric worried about you." The words tumbled out of his mouth.

"Eric let *me* worry about me. He only worried about himself." Even before he'd started doing drugs, Eric had always been lost in his own world.

Quinn sighed. "Eric loved you."

I nodded because that was true. Eric had loved me as much as I'd loved him. "That doesn't mean you have to look out for me," I said, my voice still low. I wasn't trying to start an argument. I just didn't want to be Quinn's responsibility. Eric had loved me, had been my best friend, but that didn't mean Quinn had to take up where Eric had left off. He couldn't, and it wasn't supposed to work like that.

Quinn pressed his hands together and cracked his knuckles. "I just don't want you to think that you can go right with Bellamy where things went wrong with Eric. He's . . ." He paused and changed tack. "You can't fix him."

It was like he'd thrown a blanket over me and tried to smother me with it. He thought he was protecting me. For whatever reason, he thought I actually needed to hear those words, and I knew, in the part of my mind that was still thinking logically, that he meant them as a kindness. But I was frozen, my spine a ramrod under my skin. I was weighed down and numb.

I wanted to say that I didn't want to fix Bellamy, that I only liked him, that I liked that he was so much more of a person and less of a rock star than I'd ever imagined. A musician and a man and not the fantasy I'd always held, and he was better that way. I wanted to tell Quinn that I didn't have a hero complex, that I would be the last person who thought he could fix someone. But I was getting snagged on what else Quinn had said.

"What do you mean?"

Quinn's expression went entirely blank, and I knew he was going to brush me off.

"Don't," I said before he could say anything himself. I held up a hand. "You can't hint around like that, and then not tell me. God, between you and Bellamy . . . What fixing do you think he needs?"

His mouth quirked up at the corner, but I couldn't tell if it was a happy expression or a rueful one. "It's not a secret. It's not that dramatic. But it's still not mine to tell, either." He leaned forward, standing up straight and moving away from the bus. "Don't you want to hear it from Bellamy instead, anyway?"

I didn't have to think about it for long. If there was something to learn about Bellamy, anything, I didn't want someone else to tell me. I wanted to learn it myself, or have Bellamy talk to me about it. I nodded. "He won't tell me, though."

Quinn stepped in front of me. "I think he will." He squinted into the sun like he was trying to tell what time it was. "Maybe he's not ready yet." Then he shrugged. "Maybe he won't ever be. It's not personal."

I nodded again. I knew it wasn't. I just . . . wanted it to be. I wanted Bellamy to want to be with me, wanted him to want to be close, and I wanted him to feel comfortable enough to tell me things. But really, we hadn't known each other that long, no matter how amazing, how intense, it had felt to kiss him, to lie beside him. And I couldn't expect him to give me his secrets so easily.

I pushed it out of my mind and followed Quinn back to the gear so we could start setting up.

X

I ran into Bellamy before the show started. The opening band was about to go on, and everyone else was hanging out just off the stage, getting ready for the show, meeting each other. Bellamy wasn't there, though, and I'd poked around through the back dressing rooms until I found him. He was sitting in front of a mirror, a vanity table in front of him. He'd put his eyeliner on, a fine black tracery that made his hazel eyes wider and bolder. But when I came into the room and he looked up, looked at my reflection behind him in the mirror, that eyeliner made him seem young and alone, a mask that didn't hide anything.

I shut the door behind me and leaned against it. Took a deep breath. Told myself that it was okay to worry, that I didn't have to be nervous about caring for someone. "All right?" He didn't seem all right. I didn't know what was wrong. But I knew there was something. I'd have to have been an idiot not to see it.

The lights were too bright in here. He was too pale under them. I imagined that if I stared hard enough, I'd be able to see the blue veins under his skin, the translucent white of his cheekbones.

He nodded but didn't turn around. We were looking at each other, but it felt like we were at a remove, separated by something that kept us safe from each other.

"Were you looking for me?" he asked.

I shrugged, not wanting to admit it, but then nodded.

He blinked, slow. Then he took a deep breath, like he was steadying himself.

"I talked with Tuck. We hadn't really . . . not since that night you heard us arguing. I think he's still angry with me," he said, simply. Plainly. "We're fine. I just . . . I don't want him angry with me."

"Oh." I didn't know what else to say. "I'm sorry. I don't think he's angry with you, Bellamy. I think he just wants to make sure you're okay." I still hadn't moved from my spot by the door.

"I know that." He flicked his hand up. "I'm worried about the next album. And he doesn't want me to worry. That's all. He's being kind. But he thinks he can stop the worry just by . . . telling me to stop. He thinks everything will be fine and there's no reason to even consider it not. But I can't . . . My brain doesn't work that way, you know? But I told him I was sorry. I think we'll be okay. I think we are."

"Bellamy." I stepped forward. He glanced down, breaking our gaze in the mirror. I moved again, walking until I was right behind him, staring down at his hair, just long enough to curl around his ears, at his slumped shoulders, at his hands clamped on the edge of the table. "Bellamy," I said again, softer.

He looked up again, caught my eye. He leaned back until his head hit my chest, the solid weight of him resting on my sternum. The breath shuddered out of my lungs. I never expected it, when he touched me, even though he'd done it time and again now, and I never knew quite how to respond to it. I raised my hands and set them on his shoulders, and when he smiled a little, I flexed my fingers. He was solid and warm under my palms. When he leaned on me, he made me feel like I was steady and strong enough to take his weight and his worries, and the idea that he thought the same thing lit me up, made me believe it might possibly be true.

He shook his head a tiny bit. I felt the movement against me more than I saw it. "Just . . . I just want to be on tour and not worry about writing right now. Like Tuck. But I have to."

He shrugged, and his mouth turned down at the corners. I thought about what Quinn had said that afternoon, about him needing to be fixed. I didn't think he'd really meant it like that, didn't think Quinn thought anyone needed fixing. But he'd meant something. I watched Bellamy's reflection. He seemed to be trying to convince himself that he was fine, trying to tell himself he was overreacting. But then he closed his eyes, and he slumped even more against me.

"I wish I could stay here with you."

I didn't know what to say to that. No soothing words came to mind. I couldn't tell him he could, that he didn't have to go out there if he didn't want to, because he did. He had the dream job that kids fantasized about and adults envied, but that didn't mean it wasn't still a job.

"You don't," I said. "I know you want to go out there and play. That's not what you're afraid of." It struck me, while I was saying it, while I looked down on the slight wave of his hair, that he *was* afraid. I blinked and met his eyes in the reflection in the mirror, and I could see it on his face. "It's okay. It's okay to . . . not want it, tonight. But I think you might feel better if you play. I'll see you out there. And we can meet right here afterward. Okay?" I didn't know if he'd want me here afterward. Maybe he'd want to be alone. Or maybe he'd want someone else. But he could tell me, if that was the case.

He nodded and drew in a deep breath, as if he was gathering himself. And when he let it out, he pulled away from me a little, held up his own weight. "Okay. You'll be here?"

I nodded. "Yup."

I stayed with him until he had to go on. He was as beautiful and magnetic as always on stage. Maybe even more so. He was alight and poured everything inside him into the crowd. When his fingers moved over the guitar strings, it was like they were flying, like he didn't even have to touch them to make music. When he leaned over the edge of the stage, swayed toward the audience, he took my breath away. He looked like he was a second away from flight, or collapse, or both, sweat pouring down his throat, his shirt stuck to him, his fingers shaking where they gripped the microphone. Like he was one second, one song, away from coming apart, shattering into a million sparkling pieces.

After the last song of the encore, while the crowd was still screaming for Escaping Indigo to come back, Bellamy handed me his guitar and disappeared. I wanted to say something to him, but there wasn't time. I had to set down Bellamy's guitar and go start figuring out where to direct people, what to pack first. Ava came back after a few minutes and helped me break down the drum set, but Tuck and Bellamy didn't reappear.

Ava left me and Quinn to pack the last of the gear into the trailer, and for a few minutes, my mind was all about the puzzle of making sure everything fit and was buffered against getting jostled or bumped. I'd been packing up the gear for a couple of weeks now, but no matter how many times I tried to do it exactly the same way, the way I knew would work, it always seemed like there was something that suddenly decided it didn't want to fit. I wrestled with the stuff, shoving at drum cases to get an extra inch of space, pulling guitar crates back and forth, until everything was snug and perfect.

I was tired when I was done, and part of me only wanted to go back to the bus and crawl into my bunk, and sleep. But I'd promised Bellamy, and the thought of seeing him was enough to get me moving again. I headed into the theater again, through the back entrance. The building was mostly quiet now, and dark, the last few people cleaning up, a couple of security guards wandering around.

I knocked on the door to the dressing room and waited for Bellamy to say I could come in before I pushed it open. He was standing this time, a towel in his hand that he was running over his hair. He had showered and was still damp, his shirt clinging to his skin. The lighting was awful, yellowy and dim while somehow being too bright at the same time, showing off all the dirty corners of the room. But I thought, standing there, that he looked beautiful. Not glittery and stunning and otherworldly like he did when he was onstage, when he was being Bellamy the Rock Star, but sweet and warm and real. His hair was sticking up every which way. He still had flecks of makeup around his eyes, like he hadn't washed his face quite enough. And he was lovely.

I shut the door behind me, and he dropped the towel and reached out his hand for me. The room wasn't very big—it only took me a step and a half to cross it, to get to him. He kept his hand out for me, and when I got close enough, he wrapped it around the back of my neck and drew me in until we were flush against each other. We kissed, and it felt like the most natural thing ever. I shut my eyes, blocked out the little room, and focused on Bellamy, kissing Bellamy, knowing he needed, in this second, me.

There was a sharp knock on the door, and we both jumped, and then we both giggled, embarrassed. Bellamy didn't let me go. I still had my hands balled in his shirt. He leaned his forehead against mine.

"Yeah?" he called out.

A muffled voice came through the door saying we needed to go, that they were locking up. Bellamy called back that we were on our way. He pressed one more kiss to my mouth, then pulled away.

He had his bag ready to go. When I turned to walk out, though, he caught my hand. He held it while I opened the door and he turned the lights off, while we walked down the hall together.

When we got out the back door, he pulled me against the wall of the building, and we kissed under the orange glow of a streetlight. Moths were fluttering around the lamp, and their blurry shadows crossed Bellamy's face, large, soft wings covering his eyes, his mouth. I kissed over them, ran my thumbs over the places they passed on his cheeks, chasing the shadows of them on his skin.

"Come on." He tugged me forward. He sounded breathless and full of want, and I couldn't quite believe that it was me who'd done that to him, who got to do that to him.

He led me to the bus. It was dark inside, only a light on a side table left on for us. I was surprised at how quiet it was. I couldn't tell if everyone had gone out, or if it was later than I'd thought, if Bellamy and I had spent more time kissing in the dressing room than I'd realized, and everyone was already asleep. I didn't care. Bellamy dropped his bag and led me over to one of the couches along the side of the bus, and we fell onto it in a tangle of legs and arms. Bellamy sprawled over me, and I could feel his heart beating under my palm, the steady, too quick pulse of it.

We were frantic. Bellamy lay over me, between my legs, and for a second I worried he'd knee me in an unfortunate place, or I'd get him in the ribs with an elbow. But we were too busy to be careful. He yanked at my shirt, pulling it up enough so that he could slide his hands over my chest. His lips moved down, kissing along my jaw, my neck, and then right back to my mouth. He tasted warm and sweet, of soda and exhaustion and, underneath, the bitter tang of the smoke from a fog machine. He tasted like I was delving into a concert come to life. I liked it, liked how odd it was, but I liked it even better when he opened his mouth wider, twisted his tongue around mine, and I tasted just him. Just Bellamy.

His hands slid around me, pressed against my back. I tugged on his waist until our hips bumped together.

"Bellamy," I said, pulling my mouth away enough to speak. I pressed harder against him. My fingers were digging into the muscles of his waist. He'd have bruises. I raised my head and kissed the spot where his neck met his shoulder, just exposed by his T-shirt. I bit down, sucked at his skin. He made a moan that went all the way through me, low and long and desperate. His fingers scrabbled against my back, my ribs.

I leaned forward, and we kissed again, as hard as before. My hands moved to his hips, to the front of his jeans, my fingers curling around the fabric. His own fingers skimmed the hollows near my hips, the dip of my waist. I couldn't breathe. I couldn't think about anything except his touch, his skin on my skin, the sounds he was making into my mouth. I hooked my fingers into his jeans, yanking the button open and unzipping so I could shove them down.

He was bare underneath them. I skimmed my fingers over the delicate skin, down until I brushed his cock. He sucked in a breath, sharp, urgent. I wanted to stop, to ask why now, what had changed his mind. I wanted to ask if, in the morning, he'd push me away again. I wanted to know if this was only a one-time thing, if I was one more fan in a string of fans. I wanted to know if, afterward, he'd still want me. I wanted to ask if he was sure.

But then he was reaching for my jeans, grabbing at them like he was desperate, and all the questions and worries I had flew out of my mind in the face of how badly I wanted him. Wanted to be close to him.

I almost yelled when he finally brought us together, but some part of my brain reminded me that we weren't really alone, that even if no one could see us, there were possibly four other people not twenty feet away. I bit my lip, hard, at the feel of soft skin on skin, at how hot and smooth he was against me. He pulled his mouth away from mine and dropped his head to my shoulder, his hands clutching at me, his breath coming in gasps. I pressed my hand to his collarbone, high enough to feel the sharp slope where his neck met his shoulder, to feel it under my fingertips when he swallowed.

I took us both in my palm and rubbed up, once. He groaned, and I did the same. He was like velvet against me, damp and warm and strong, and so intimate that it made me shake. It was like I had never been quite so close to anyone, and I forgot where I was, forgot to be careful. Forgot that we were still mostly dressed. He felt naked against me, and I felt like I was completely bare to him.

"Micah." My name was a whimper in his mouth. He shifted, just a little. He brought a hand up and licked his palm, and then his hand joined mine, slick and wet. We stroked together. It was still too rough, our skin catching, our rhythm not in sync, but we didn't stop. I couldn't, and I didn't think he could either. He kept his head down, our cheeks together, our hands tangled at our groins and our chests.

I squeezed harder, sliding my palm over the tips of our cocks. Bellamy moaned, louder, rougher this time, and tipped his head back. I shifted the hand at his collar, pressing down on the sharp curve of bone, my thumb skimming the hollow of his throat. He opened his eyes and stared at me. I kept moving my other hand over us, pushing us together in a way that felt almost too close, too intimate, all that hidden skin aligned. Up and down, faster and harder, and his lips trembled. A whimper of sound, almost a plea, escaped him, but he didn't close his eyes again, didn't look away from me.

He came in a rush of warmth over my hips, and I followed a few seconds later. We lay there, panting, my fingers still around us, our bodies still pressed hard together, my palm still at his throat. He hadn't taken his eyes off me. He blinked, slowly, his heart thudding in an unsteady pattern under the heel of my hand.

"Micah," he said, his tone almost cautious.

I sighed and closed my eyes. I kept one arm locked around his back, and he held me just as tight. The aftermath was almost more intense than the sex itself had been, and it made me want to shiver or tuck myself in against him or hold him hard enough that he'd know I meant it when I said I wanted to be with him.

I opened my eyes and smiled. I was so nervous. "Hey."

He smiled back, and a rush of relief washed through me. "Hey. You okay?"

I nodded. I still didn't want to move, but with my eyes open, it was pretty obvious that we were in a precarious position. I was sticky, and I needed to wipe my hand on something that wasn't the couch. I flailed around until I found my T-shirt, and rubbed the fabric between my fingers. I passed it to Bellamy, and he did the same.

"Bellamy . . ." I wasn't sure what I wanted to ask him, or how well I could get my brain to connect to my mouth right now. I was kind of dazed. Sex hadn't felt that intense in . . . I couldn't even remember. Never, maybe. It was like a splash of color in the dark, so bright and vivid I wanted to keep rolling it over and over in my mind, remembering it.

Bellamy kissed me, soft and gentle, then again, like he didn't want to stop or pull away. He ran his fingers through my hair and smoothed it down. "Can we talk in the morning?"

I nodded. Better that way, yeah. We stood up and put ourselves back together enough that, if anyone came out of one of the bunks or the back, we wouldn't be completely mortified. I should probably be mortified anyway. I didn't feel it right then, though. I felt lazy and content and blissed out.

Bellamy kissed me once more when we got to our bunks. I thought briefly about asking him to sleep next to me again, but I was all tangled up in feelings, and he probably was too. He might need a while to himself as much as I did. He disappeared into his bunk, pulling the curtain behind him, and I went to mine.

chapter eight

t he next morning, I rolled out of bed and nearly smacked right into Ava. She eyed me up and down, taking in my hair all sticking up on one side, the places on my face and neck that were probably red from where Bellamy's scruff had rubbed. Her eyebrows rose until I thought they'd disappear into her hair.

"Wild night?" She wasn't smiling, and there wasn't any levity in the words.

"I . . ."

She waved her hand like she was swatting away a fly. "Don't bother. I heard you. The whole bus heard you."

Dear god. I tried to work up some more embarrassment, but there was only a flicker. Seemed I was fresh out. "Sorry."

She nodded, then switched and shook her head. "Are you and he . . .?" She did the eyebrow thing again.

I hesitated. "I don't know." I didn't. That was the truth, at least.

"Oh." She drew the sound out. I *really* did not want to be standing here between the bunks, having this conversation with Ava. My face must be on fire. I wanted to escape, go brush my teeth, put actual clothes on.

"Do you want to be . . .?" she asked. So much hinting and poking at things. I was starting to wish we'd all just come out and say what we meant, what we felt, what we wanted, instead of this goddamn hinting around.

"Yes," I said, surprising us both with how firm the word came out. "Yes, I do," I repeated, softer.

She nodded. She opened her mouth, but seemed to think better of it, and then had to stop and consider what she wanted to say.

"Be careful," she said finally. "I don't want him hurt. And I don't want you hurt either."

I sighed. "That's the plan."

She reached out and touched my arm. "Seriously. He doesn't . . . He can't snap back from that kind of thing. It's not in him."

I nodded, but before I could say anything, something heavy landed on my shoulder. I glanced around, and there was Bellamy, his chin resting on me. I leaned back a little, and he braced himself so he could take my weight.

"Leave him alone," Bellamy told Ava.

She tilted her head to the side. "What are you doing?"

He shook his head, his chin digging into my shoulder. "It's none of your business."

She widened her eyes, shrugged, and moved past us. Her hand flicked out, and she gave him a sharp tap on the waist. It could have been a *Don't mess this up* tap, or a *Good for you.* Knowing Ava, and the way she knew Bellamy, it was probably something of both.

As soon as she was gone, I shifted, and Bellamy moved back a step. I didn't know whether to turn and face him and try to talk to him, or pretend that nothing at all had happened. I didn't know if he'd want to pretend that. I didn't want that, I realized. I really, really didn't. I wanted to at least talk about it. If I was being optimistic, I wanted it to happen again. But Bellamy had a way of pulling away when I tried to reach for him. It might be better if I just crossed my fingers and hoped he'd come to me.

I reached for my bunk and hauled myself up so I could sit. He moved over right away and folded his arms on the mattress. He rested his chin on them and looked up at me through his lashes, like he had that first night he'd come to me, when we'd talked about my tattoo.

"How much of that did you hear?" I asked him.

"Not much to hear."

"No."

He hesitated, then swung himself around so he was sitting beside me, our legs dangling together. The edges of our pinky fingers almost touched on the bed.

"I came to find you," he said.

"Yeah?" I asked, letting my tone hint that I wanted him to elaborate.

He didn't. "Yeah."

I let myself fall backward into the bunk. My legs still stuck out, and the bunk wasn't deep enough for me to lie back, so I had to bend my body behind his. It was strange to be so close to him again, after the night before. It should have been so easy to reach out for him now, but it seemed harder than ever. It was as if all that intimacy had created a wall instead of breaking one down.

"Do you want to talk about last night?" I asked, finally. I'd told myself I wasn't going to do it, but I couldn't not. I had to . . . get it out there. Say *something*. I'd been tired of this impasse with Bellamy before we'd slept together, and I didn't think I could live with it at all now. He could so easily tell me it couldn't happen again. But at least I'd know then. At least I wouldn't be left wondering.

"No."

Or he could say that. I closed my eyes. I didn't, honestly, have any idea of where to go from here.

I heard him take a deep breath, and opened my eyes. In the shadowy murk of the bunk, I could just see his shoulders rise and fall. "No, I don't want to talk about it. But I need . . . There's stuff I have to say anyway. We have to say." He paused, as if he didn't quite know where to start. "I liked last night, Micah. A lot."

I shouldn't have been that relieved, maybe, to hear that, but I was. It didn't really mean anything, I reminded myself, so as not to get my hopes up. But it did mean something. It meant something to me, even if that was as far as it ever went.

"Me too. A lot." I kept my voice soft. I didn't want to make him skittish. I was afraid he'd give up and walk away.

He turned toward me a tiny bit. His head was bowed. I couldn't see anything but the very edge of his face, a thin profile of him, from back here. "Would you . . . I mean, I'd like . . ." I didn't think I'd ever heard him so flustered. "Do you want that to happen again?"

Blunt, I could deal with. Blunt, I was happy with. "Yes," I said, deciding playing coy might be more comfortable, but it would be the worst option here. "I would, Bellamy. Very much."

He took a deep breath. "There are some things I need to tell you."

My heart tripped over itself. "Okay."

He was quiet for a long minute, and I thought he was gathering himself, trying to decide what to say.

"Sometimes you look at me like you're afraid of me. You look at me like I'm . . . something special. I can't live up to that, Micah. I'm not."

We'd been over this. Over and over. It was beginning to dawn on me that maybe Bellamy was the type of person who'd need to go over it a thousand times before he believed what I said, or believed himself. Study it from every angle, so he could trust what I told him.

I raised my hand, let it hover over his back, my fingers not quite touching the fabric of his shirt. He held so still under my hand, like he could feel me there.

"When I was in the band with Eric," I said, because I didn't know how else to explain, "I wanted to be your equal."

He flinched, and my fingers brushed him. I yanked my hand away, but he settled, leaning back the tiniest bit. After a second, I touched him again, laid my hand flat against his lower back. I could feel the bumps of his vertebrae under my palm.

"I mean, I wanted all the other things too. To be successful. Be a rock star. Money. Adoring fans." I laughed to myself. "I wanted to have leftover sushi in the fridge."

He tried to turn, to see me. "What?"

"You know, when you go out for sushi, but it's expensive, so you can only order a little bit?" He hesitated, then nodded. Maybe he didn't know. Maybe he made enough money to order all the ten-dollar sushi rolls he wanted. "I always wanted to be able to order a lot, more than I could eat, so the next day, there'd be leftover sushi in the fridge." Eric and I had never had sushi before we'd started driving into the nearest cities to play shows. When we were out, before a show, we always tried to eat somewhere that served something we'd never had before. Sushi had been our favorite, though. Eric had loved to wave the chopsticks around while he talked. A lot of the time, when I thought of him, I pictured him sitting at our favorite sushi restaurant, one elbow on the bar in front of him, chopsticks dancing through the air while he made a point, the sticky ends clicking together.

"Sushi's not so great on the second day," Bellamy mumbled.

"Yeah." He didn't say it like he was trying to teach me anything, though. He didn't say it like he was trying to discredit what I wanted. He said it like maybe he got what I meant. Even if second-day sushi wasn't his benchmark for success. "Mostly we just wanted to make enough to keep doing it, you know?" I said, going back to the main point of the conversation. "But I always wanted to do it so that I could be your equal too. So that if we ever met, I could be proud of myself when I faced you. I could be somebody instead of nobody in front of you."

He tilted his head around so he could catch my eyes. "You're my equal, Micah. You've never been nobody."

"I know." I nodded against the bedspread. "Logically, I know that. It's just, sometimes . . . I wish I'd done better before I met you. I wish you hadn't met me as . . . just the roadie. I wish I'd been someone who could stand even with you." It hadn't only been Bellamy. It had been all of the musicians I'd respected, the artists. Ava, and Tuck, and people in other bands I loved. I'd wanted to stand on their level. I'd wanted to be able to be proud of myself among them, whether I actually ever met any of them or not. Bellamy had always been at the top of that list, though. He had always been the unattainable dream, the image I clung to. Now here he was, and here I was, and we wanted each other. And we were both too afraid that we wouldn't measure up in the other's eyes. It was ridiculous. And it wasn't ridiculous at all, because it felt too important and too big to mess up, and it would be too painful if we did.

"Do you need me to be perfect for you?" I moved my fingers, the tiniest bit, down the ridge of his spine. I wished I'd touched him more last night. Gotten my hands all over him, felt the skin on his back and his chest and his legs. I wished it hadn't been rushed. I wished we'd been somewhere private, just the two of us, somewhere bigger than the tiny bus couch. "Do you need me to . . . be that person who has a record deal and is exactly on your level? When we were together last night, did you care that I was your roadie? Did you care that you were Bellamy of Escaping Indigo? Did any of that matter?"

He shook his head. The movement was slow and thoughtful, like he was trying to take in what I was saying.

"I don't want you to be . . . crazy perfect." Then I laughed. "Don't get me wrong, Bellamy. Sometimes I'm so nervous around you, sometimes I remember who you are, and who I am, and I know I can't ever measure up to that. I remember that you're a rock star and I'm a roadie, and I can't figure out what I'm thinking, that I could ever be with someone like you. That someone like you would want me."

"I do want you, though." The words were soft, but quick and sure, and they made my heart squeeze in my chest.

"That's my point," I said back. "I want you. I like Bellamy the Rock Star. But I don't want to be with you because of that. That's only a part of you. I'm never going to be the musician who can stand even with you. But I think maybe that matters a lot less than I thought. When we were together last night . . . none of that mattered, Bellamy. It was just us."

For a minute, a long minute, I thought Bellamy wasn't going to say anything. Wasn't going to take the opening I was offering. That he'd brush it all off again, or that, maybe, he'd finally get up and leave, and that would be it. We would go back to whatever we'd been before I'd met him outside that venue for a smoke in the dark. Acquaintances. Coworkers.

Maybe it had been a mistake. Maybe I shouldn't have been here at all. It had taken me so long to pick up my drumsticks again, to sit down and play anything, because I had felt so hollow, and the sound of my drums had only seemed to echo around in that space inside me. Too loud. Too sharp. I'd just gotten back into it when Quinn had offered me the job as roadie. And now it wasn't only the drumming, but all of this, the music and the touring and everything that could have been, all in my face, day after day. Maybe it was all too soon, too many almost familiar things in a situation that wasn't familiar at all, too many wants and things I knew I didn't want, and now this, added on top.

I was lonely. I was lost and confused and missing someone so badly it was like I had a hole in my life that I would never be able to fill in. I *wanted*, and more than that, I needed. Needed other people around me to remind me that when Eric died, I hadn't gone with him. Needed someone to be straight with me. Needed someone to treat me like I wasn't unimportant, like I mattered. And somewhere between falling asleep with Bellamy beside me and talking to him when he could have talked with anyone, just enjoying the time I had with him, the time I'd thought he'd enjoyed too, I'd started to think Bellamy could be that person. And I wanted him, now, to say something that would tell me I hadn't been wrong. Anything.

"Right." He took a deep breath. I sat up, slowly, and turned so I could see him. And then we sat there, waiting, at some weird standoff where he tore down the walls I used to protect myself and he didn't know it hurt. Where he made me feel wanted and didn't realize how much that meant to me. Where I told him he didn't have to be perfect for me to love him, and he didn't believe it.

"Listen," he said. "I don't want you to know me. I don't want to tell you things. I don't want you to think of me as anyone but Bellamy the singer who plays decent guitar in a really great band. I want to be all shiny in your eyes."

I laughed, and it didn't sound amused at all. "Then what are you doing crawling into my bunk? Or sleeping with me? Or holding my hand like you did, because, fuck, Bellamy, I thought that meant something. It felt like it did. And it didn't mean me seeing you as just a singer."

He shook his head and stared up at the ceiling, like all the answers were there and he only had to pull them down. Then he looked down at his hands. "I *like* being shiny and special for you. I like the way you look at me like I'm something awesome."

I narrowed my eyes at him. "You mean you like the way fans look at you."

"Yes!" He laughed, but I didn't, and he hurried on. "But I don't . . . I don't want you to be a fan, Micah. I mean, I do, but I don't want that to be all. I want . . . you. Just you." He sighed and glanced up at me through his eyelashes, and it melted me a little, because he was so beautiful. I looked away. "I don't get to keep that stuff if I keep hiding myself from you, do I? If I want to be perfect for you, I don't get all the things about you I want. I don't get to hold your hand and reach for you if I'm hiding things."

I kept my eyes down on the comforter. I was bunching it up between my fingers, twisting the fabric around and around. "No."

He sighed, and it sounded like he was exhaling worry and fear and everything that had made it hard for him to tell me anything, tell me what was going on, tell me why he kept holding me at arm's length.

"I don't . . . I don't work the way everybody else does. There's something . . . There's something wrong with me. Anxiety or something. I don't really know. It's just . . . a thing. And it makes it . . . It makes everything more difficult. Makes me worry. Makes me worry until I'm sick, makes me rethink everything, makes me afraid to trust anyone. I can't . . ." He trailed off. "It's just a thing I do. But it makes everything . . . hurt."

"Okay." I'd heard of anxiety. It wasn't that uncommon. I didn't really know anything about it, but I didn't think it made people undateable jerks, either. I didn't get why this was a big deal. I didn't get why it was the thing coming between us, why it was something Bellamy felt he needed to hide.

He turned to me. His eyes were right on mine now, his gaze intense, serious. He reached out and grabbed my wrist, holding it tight, until I thought I could feel the imprint of his fingers against my bones. "Whatever you're thinking . . . You're downplaying it in your mind. I can see it. And that's fine, but it's not right. It's not . . . the truth. This thing . . . It makes me hard to be with, Micah. Very hard. It makes me . . . sad and unpleasant and unkind, and very much not perfect."

I jerked my wrist back, pulling away from him. He let his hand drop to the mattress. "I never wanted you to be perfect. Only honest. Why didn't you just tell me?"

His expression hardened, went flat and angry. "Because." He waved a hand around his head. "This is something broken inside me. I should fucking have control over my mind, Micah, you know? And I don't. It's . . . I'm . . ."

"What?" I frowned too, and shook my head. "What? You're ashamed? Embarrassed? That's ridiculous."

He slapped his hand down against the bed, hard. "I'm scared! And it's not ridiculous at all. And fuck you for thinking so."

I sat back, stunned, and clamped my mouth shut, my jaw so tight I thought I'd snap something.

"I'm scared," he said, softer, but no less angry, "that I can't trust you, that I can't trust myself. That you'll see this thing in me and you'll think I'm crazy, and you'd be right. I am. I don't have control. I'm not perfect. I want to be, for you, so badly. But I'll have to keep hiding things from you, keep pretending, if I want you to see me that way. And . . . part of me doesn't want to pretend anymore. Part of me wants to let you see, because I know you already do, and I'm not good at hiding it anymore. But more because . . . it's real. This flaw, it's the truth of me." He took a shaky breath. "And I know that that's hard for people to deal with, I know it makes me unlikeable, I know no one wants that in their boyfriend . . ."

He trailed off, and something clicked for me.

"That's what happened. Isn't it? That's why your boyfriend left. Because of this, specifically. Because he wanted you to be perfect and he didn't understand why you weren't."

Bellamy closed his eyes. "You don't . . . You haven't seen what I get like."

"Obviously not!" I burst out. A laugh spilled from me, and it sounded harsh and raw and awful. "You wouldn't let me see it. Of course I don't know!"

It was Bellamy who sat back and clapped his mouth shut this time.

"Bellamy." I tried to be gentler. I wanted to shake him, to tell him it didn't matter, to tell him he could trust me. Instead I took deep breaths, and tried to be calm. My hand pressed down over his on the mattress. His fingers were trembling. "Do you honestly . . . Do you honestly think I care? If you're difficult? If you're not always . . ." I waved my other hand at him. "Always a rock star? I know you're a man too."

"You didn't. At first. Maybe not even now. You looked at me like I was something else."

I swallowed. I didn't know what to say, because he was right. He'd been this amazing creature, something ethereal and not quite real, and I'd let myself worship him. And I'd let myself think he was better than me, because I'd believed it. Maybe still did believe it. Because he was Bellamy and I was just some kid from a shitty town, who didn't even know what I was made of. What to do with my life anymore.

I stared at Bellamy while he looked down at his feet, dangling over the edge of the mattress. He didn't look anything like he had that day a couple of weeks ago, when I'd first spoken to him, when the conversation between us had been nothing like I'd expected. He had seemed so very far away from me then, like no matter how close I sat, we'd never really touch. He had been a distant star, cold and hard and glittering. And now he was rough around the edges, unpolished, desperate even. But he was warm and alive and right here, right in front of me, and he was leaning toward me, offering himself up to me, like he wanted us to collide.

I let us, moving enough that we touched down one side. His hip was a sharp point against mine. His toes were wedged up against my foot. It was only a tiny brush of contact. One edge of him against one edge of me. But right then, it felt like a lot. Better, more intimate in a way I couldn't define, than when we'd had sex.

He breathed in, and I could feel it, could feel the tension all down his arm and his side as he inhaled, like a thick current on his skin.

"Where does this leave us?" he asked, and I was taken aback for a second, because he was the one asking. He was asking me, leaving it up to me.

I shook my head. "I didn't want the version of you I can get by listening to your CDs and searching you on the internet, Bellamy. I've *had* that. It's awesome. But I'm here now. I want something real, you know?"

He nodded, but he still looked hesitant, unsure, like he was seriously considering getting ready to bolt.

I was almost considering letting him. I hadn't been expecting any of this. I hadn't even expected Bellamy to actually want me. And this, now, felt . . . serious. Obviously it couldn't be that serious, since we'd really only met a few weeks ago. But he'd told me what he'd been hiding. He'd given me something that made him feel fragile and less than and vulnerable. He had trusted me with it, and I had to be careful with it, with him. And that was serious.

"You wanted me last night," I said, my voice soft.

I glanced over at him, and he rolled his eyes at me. "What part gave that away, Micah? The part where I jumped you on the couch? Or was it when I couldn't wait to get your jeans all the way off?"

It was enough to surprise a laugh out of me. I was still leaning against him. His hand was still in mine. I moved his, so his palm was up and I could twine our fingers together. "No. Well, I mean, yes. But . . ." I pulled in a breath and held it, tried to make it steady me. It didn't really work. "I mean, you wanted me to come find you, after the show. Me. Right? You waited for me." I felt myself blushing. "I mean, that sounds really vain and snobby. Maybe anyone else would have worked too, but you needed—"

He held up a hand. "I wanted you. You, Micah."

"Why?" I wasn't trying to get him to say anything. I only, honestly, wanted to know. I didn't understand it, and I wanted it to make sense.

He shrugged. "I don't know." He tightened his hand on mine. "Because you told me you'd come back after. Because you knew what to say to make me feel better. Because when you draw me, it's like you actually catch part of me on the paper. I don't know, Micah."

That was definitely more than I'd expected, and for a second, I just sat there, bowled over by how easily he'd said all that. I wanted to sit with it for a while and let it soak in. I didn't think I'd ever had a conversation like this before in my life. I wasn't sure I ever wanted to have another. It had been so draining, even though it had been good too.

"Do you still want me there, when you're done with a show?" I wasn't trying to whisper, but my voice came out so quiet and raw. I couldn't make it any louder. "You could have anyone, Bellamy." I laughed, and it sounded as wrecked and raw as my voice. "Anyone. But if you want me, then . . ." I sighed. "I want that too. I really do." It seemed like it should have been harder, to say something like that. But after all of this, it wasn't. "And I promise I won't leave you because you're being unhappy or . . . whatever."

"You can't promise that," he said again, like he had before.

"I can promise to try." I squeezed his hand. "You only have to tell me whether you want that or not."

It didn't take him as long as I'd thought it would. It didn't take him much time at all. "I want that."

chapter nine

X

Sometimes when I thought about Eric, I wondered how I'd let myself become so wrapped up in one person. I didn't think it was wrong, how close Eric and I had been, how tangled we'd gotten in each other's lives. I wouldn't have done it differently. I knew that I wouldn't. But the untangling, the suddenness of it, had felt as if half of me had been pulled away. As if all these pieces of me had been yanked apart, scattered. And it had hurt like I'd been cut right down the middle, and he'd taken all the important parts of me with him, wherever he'd gone. Sometimes I thought of myself as the leftovers. The scraps of his life, and the scraps of mine where he used to be.

It had been a long time since I'd had anything new, anything that was just mine, and not a piece of Eric too. But Bellamy felt like that, and I liked it.

For the next several days, everything was . . . easy. It was as if something had been fixed between me and Bellamy, like the air had been cleared, and I had this ridiculous idea in my head that nothing could go wrong now. It was pretty spectacular, to finish a show and have Bellamy look to me first, to have him come find me when he wanted to cuddle, to slip into his bunk some nights, to curl up so tight with him so neither of us fell off the narrow mattress. I felt good—wanted and cared for and as if I was doing a halfway decent job of caring for him. I loved being with him. I liked the job I was doing. I liked being with the band. They were the only things that seemed important, and everything outside of our world of touring and tour bus and music and friends seemed insignificant.

We drove from Atlanta to New Orleans, and played a date in the French Quarter. I was the only one who hadn't been there before, and we ended up walking around until the wee hours of the morning. I liked the city best when the sun was just coming up, and everything was watery pink and blue, the fresh air cool and smelling of the Mississippi River. It was a different place than the wild, ongoing party it had been after the sun went down, but there was still something special about it, something that made it different than anywhere else I'd ever been. I hadn't believed, before, that there could really be a magic to a place, but I thought maybe there was in New Orleans. I didn't want to leave.

After that we headed into Texas, which was boring as fuck to stare out the window at, and played a date in Houston, at a festival the local radio station was putting on. It wasn't as crazy as playing Coachella or Lollapalooza, which Escaping Indigo had played earlier in the summer, or any other huge festival. It was only two stages, with a handful of popular bands, instead of a half-dozen stages with Paul McCartney at the end of the night. They weren't even headlining. But it was still a big deal, and the band was excited about it.

I was excited too—for the band, and for getting to hang out at a festival. Eric and I had always marked our summers by how many shows we saw, how many weekends were taken up with endless concerts under the sun or the rain. All those days we'd spent driving from place to place, sometimes days away, to see all the bands we loved. There was something that made a festival different than any other concert. An atmosphere that was charged. It always felt, to me, that I was connected to all these other people in the most normal but also the most incredible way. We were all there for the same thing. We were all riding the same energy frequency, and you could feel it. It reminded me of the festivals I'd gone to as a teenager, how they had made me feel as if I was escaping into something, like I could stand in the middle of them and wrap the music around me. Like I was free for a few hours.

It didn't hurt that this particular festival was happening on a gorgeous day, still warm enough to be summer but slipping over enough into nearly-fall weather that no one was passing out from the heat. I'd been to Texas before and mostly remembered it being hot and brown, but the venue was an open park, surrounded by huge shade trees, the concert-goers standing on deep-green grass. Setting up was rushed, and Quinn and I were a bit panicky about getting everything up on the stage as quickly as possible, but the set went fine, Escaping Indigo playing to a huge crowd who definitely loved them. Then it was a rush for all of us to get the gear down again. And then we were done, the whole rest of the afternoon and evening stretching out in front of us.

The band and Quinn disappeared into the groups of people backstage. There was a whole grassy area and a wide parking lot where the buses were parked, and bands and crew were all hanging out, grilling food, catching up with friends, playing the sporadic game of some weirdly aggressive Frisbee. People drifted from group to group, saying hello, grabbing a beer or a soda. It was like a family reunion, except everybody seemed to like each other.

I liked it too, and I didn't think Bellamy or Ava or anyone else would have minded me tagging along and meeting their friends. But I wanted to be in the audience. Bellamy got involved in a serious, and seriously over my head, discussion with Vix Vincent and Sawyer Bell about what a fiddle added to the mood of a song. Vix and Sawyer were members of the band Victoria Vincent—I'd heard their music and immediately fallen in love with the way they blended genres to create something that was both innovative and familiar, with Vix's lush vocals laid out over a sharp, clean rhythm section and silky-yet-edgy melodies. I was starstruck when Bellamy introduced me to them, but he made it feel easy—and it was for him. He talked to famous people day in and day out. Vix grinned at me and Sawyer threw me a polite wave and a smile, and then they both got back to the business of music.

I stood and listened to them talk for a while, and I wanted to listen some more, because how often was it that you got to sit in on a conversation like that? But the crowd and the live music were calling me, and the three of them were getting into the technical side of playing stringed instruments, which was something I didn't know too much about. I decided to head out, and said good-bye to Vix and Sawyer. Then I kissed Bellamy on the forehead and told him I'd be back. He waved like he'd heard me, although I wasn't positive. He could call me if he couldn't remember where I'd gone.

Then I snuck out, past the security guards standing at the backstage entrance. They didn't care where I went—they just didn't want to let in anyone who wasn't supposed to be back there. I remembered to tuck my crew pass into my pocket, and then I drifted past the barriers that separated the fans from the bands, where I could hear the music from the side of the stage I was more used to. Where I could look up and see a band and be nothing but another fan, getting lost in the sounds. I followed the narrow trails between people until I was in the heart of the crowd. I'd say we were dancing, but we were too crammed together. Mostly we swayed, bumping into each other, absorbing the music and breathing the same salty, tangy air. After a few songs, I started to let myself unwind, let everything go. Every time I tilted my face up to catch the breeze on my damp skin, I felt a tiny bit freer. I was surrounded by people, true, but I was completely alone. I was absorbed into a mass of music and common ground, a place where I could latch on to my real self and what I wanted and not think about anything but sweat and sound and movement.

I'd watched almost a band's whole set when my phone buzzed in my pocket. It was a text from Bellamy, asking where I was. I wrote back, telling him, as best I could, where I'd gone. I didn't know if he'd be able to find me in the crowd, but I figured I could watch the end of the set, then go meet him somewhere.

Fifteen minutes later, though, someone came up behind me. He wrapped his arms around my waist and leaned against my back. He didn't say anything, and I didn't try to either. I took a breath, breathed in all the excitement and the grass and the sweat and the smoke and the happiness around us.

We watched the band on stage like that, swaying together until the last song of the set was over, and then I turned around so I could see him. He had a hat pulled low, hiding his face enough that he'd be hard to recognize if anyone spotted him. "How'd you find me?" I asked.

He shrugged. "I just wandered around."

One stage over, another band was coming on. Their singer shouted out to the crowd, guitars twanged, and then a song started up. I didn't turn around, and Bellamy didn't look away. His hand came up, and he cupped his palm over the tattoo on my hip. I wasn't wearing a shirt, and his touch, unexpected and so, so wanted, made me shiver from my toes to my fingertips.

"Will you ever regret it?" His fingers trailed over the raised ink.

I shook my head. People had asked me that before. What if Escaping Indigo made a terrible record? What if I outgrew their music? Maybe they would, or maybe I would, although I couldn't imagine either happening. But I wouldn't regret it, either way. Their music was a part of me, had shaped me. That would always mean something to me. I would always want to wear them on my skin. Even if Bellamy and I had a huge argument, and we never spoke again. Even if the band reminded me of how awkward and uncomfortable this time had been, I wouldn't regret it. It marked a part of me, a part of my life, and nothing was going to change that.

His fingers were still moving over my skin, slower now, in expanding circles. He was watching me, and I didn't think he was paying any attention to what his hand was doing. He had this expression on his face like he couldn't quite figure me out, or like he couldn't figure out how we'd gotten here, to this exact place.

Then I moved into his hand, and he sucked in a breath and flattened his palm over my waist. I leaned forward. The new band was loud, and I had to put my lips right to his ear to be sure he heard me.

"I want to go somewhere with you. But I'll feel bad if we walk out on the end of the festival."

I stepped back, and he was smiling at me. Not just smiling, actually, but outright grinning. "I knew I liked you for a reason."

I smiled back. He made me want to smile all the time. "Music first?"

He nodded. I turned around again, tugging his arm with me, and he obliged and slid his arms around me so his hands rested against my stomach. He pulled me against him again, the fabric of his shirt soft and rough at the same time against my skin, and damp with sweat. I'd never actually watched a concert with a boyfriend before. I wasn't good at it. I was always too focused on the music, on the band and not the person with me, enough that I'd always figured it'd be a bad idea to ask a guy to go to a show with me. But it was obviously different with Bellamy, because he was as involved in the music as I was. And it was better, because we got to see it all tangled up in each other.

We watched the rest of that set together, another as the sun went down, and then the last two bands. By the time the headliner got off the stage, it was reasonably late, dark, and I was exhausted. I hadn't really done anything all day except get the band on and off the stage that afternoon, but standing in the sun all day had taken its toll.

Bellamy took my hand and started pulling me across the big expanse of grass. It was so open and empty, now that people were leaving or standing in little groups. It had been people packed shoulder to shoulder before, enough that you couldn't see the grass at all. Bellamy led us across the flow of traffic—everyone was heading toward the front gates, but he was moving me backward. I thought he'd make for the backstage space and the buses beyond that, but instead, right before we got to the security barrier, he tugged me to the side, where there was a clump of tall trees. We walked into the middle of it. He turned and pushed my back against one of the tree trunks, and kissed me until I was dizzy.

He stepped back, and I asked, breathlessly, "Don't they want to close the park?"

He shrugged, but he looked about as dazed as I felt. "I don't see anyone coming for us."

I reached up and took his hat off, and then I couldn't resist running my fingers through his hair, smoothing it back. He leaned in, and we kissed again, and then we slid down until we were sitting on the grass, my hands running over his body, his hips between my legs like he wanted me to hold on to him.

We separated for another breath, and he leaned against me, pressing his face into my shoulder. "I want to take you somewhere where we can actually lie down." His voice was muffled against my skin, his breath warm and damp. I slid my hand into his hair, held him against me. He could probably feel my heart thumping away like mad.

"That'd be nice." It'd be more than nice. I wanted to take my time with him. I wanted to see him naked, see what he looked like spread out on a bed. Even the idea of it made me nervous. He was still Bellamy, still so far out of my league it was ridiculous. But I wanted to know what sounds he'd make when I could touch him for hours instead of minutes, when we had enough room to stretch and explore.

I wanted to know how he'd look tangled up in sheets, all mussed and rumpled.

I slid my hand up the back of his shirt. "When we get home?" I meant when we were through with the tour. It wouldn't be long now. I held my breath as I asked. I tensed up, even though I didn't mean to. Bellamy and I hadn't talked about after. Our world had been the tour, the music, and I'd let myself forget everything that would come after, had let myself forget that this, the tour, the bus, this departure from normal life, would come to end. I didn't know if Bellamy had thought about it. I didn't know if he'd want to keep seeing me.

He just kissed his way across my collarbone, though. His mouth on me made me shiver. "Yeah," he said, and it was like he was trying to imprint the word on my skin. He slipped his hand lower, over my waist to the rough fabric of my jeans, and I arched into his hand. He rubbed over me, slow and almost too hard, and I heard myself moan, knew I should be embarrassed, and couldn't work up enough thought to care. All that mattered was Bellamy and me and the dark.

He stopped and gazed up at me. "Do you want . . ." He trailed off, then tried again. "We don't have to do anything. We can just make out. Or we can wait until we get back to the bus. I just thought we might get some privacy out here."

It *was* a little weird, and I was worried about what I'd be sitting on if I took my jeans off, but it actually was more private here than it would be on the bus, probably. It was quiet in the park now. The last of the stragglers were leaving, and I could hear people moving around, but they were far off. And it was gorgeous out. Just chilly enough now that a tiny shiver came over me, that I could feel the heat of Bellamy's hands wherever they moved.

"We have to be fast, though," I said. He laughed and reached up to kiss me. It was probably supposed to be a quick one, but we got caught in each other, and he tasted so good. Salty sweet, his tongue soft and lazy against mine.

I was so turned on it was almost painful. I wiggled against him, trying to get some more contact, and he dropped his head against my shoulder and groaned. His hips flexed, and I squeezed my thighs around him.

He moved down then, and I was glad, even though part of me only wanted to keep kissing him and kissing him. His mouth opened on my shoulder, at the tender space at the bottom of my neck. He kissed in an arc, his lips skimming my collarbone, his tongue dipping into the tiny indentation at the base of my throat.

It was like I wasn't in my body anymore, or maybe like I was so far in it that I could feel my consciousness in every cell. I was my skin, I was the sensation of his tongue on me, his hands gripping my waist. I was broken into pieces, tiny sections of myself that were all about Bellamy and how he felt against me, how we fit together. He lifted his head, and I met his eyes. His pupils were blown wide, black and liquid in the dark. He didn't smile, just stared at me, so intent on me, on what I was feeling.

He kept kissing down my body, taking his time, even though I'd said we would need to be fast. I didn't care anymore. This was so good it made everything else leave my mind. His hands were busy too. One held me at my waist, keeping me still, his thumb sweeping over my skin. With the other, he pulled at the waistband of my jeans, tipping it down enough that he could touch that sensitive strip of skin underneath. Then he wiggled down and kissed me there.

I arched my hips up, the movement completely involuntary. "Bellamy." My voice was ragged and soft, a scrap of torn cloth.

"Shh." He undid the button of my jeans, then the zipper, still with those slow, smooth movements, his fingers dragging across the front of my boxers before he tugged them and my jeans down. I lifted my hips for him, and he pulled the clothes to my knees.

He sat back on his heels, my legs open around him—as open as they could get while they were trapped by my jeans—and stared down at me. I felt so exposed, not only because we were in the middle of a park, a breeze wafting right over me, but because he was looking at me like that. Just sitting there and taking me in, his eyes moving over my hips and my chest to my face, and then back down. He closed his hand around my cock, sure but gentle, the tips of his fingers calloused enough from all that guitar playing that I could feel them, rough against me. He twisted his hand, cupping me and holding me in place, and bent to kiss the head.

A stream of tiny whimpers worked their way out of me. I lifted a hand and jammed my fist against my teeth. Bellamy switched from using his lips to his tongue, licking his way up, and I got lost in it. I didn't know what he was doing, couldn't sort out all the sensations, and it didn't matter. All that mattered was how incredibly good it felt and the little sounds that Bellamy was making that told me he was enjoying it almost as much as I was.

"Bellamy," I groaned. For once, my mouth wasn't running off without me, but I wished I had something else to say, some other word besides his name, some other way to plead for whatever unnameable thing it was I needed from him. I cupped my hand around the back of his neck, urging him on, my fingers digging into his skin.

He moved forward and took me farther into his mouth, and I thought I'd lose it, right at that moment. He slid his mouth back up, slow, then went back down again. He repeated the movement, again and again, before he let me slip out of his mouth, the breeze cold on my wet skin. He looked up at me, and he was grinning, his hair disheveled, falling in his eyes, his lips swollen and damp. I pushed my fingers through it, tangling them in it.

"Please," I said, and he went back down.

I tipped my head back against the tree behind me and gazed up at the sky. Through the branches and the leaves, glossy black in the dark, I could just make out the sky and the stars wheeling above us.

I looked back down at him, at my fingers in his dark hair, his mouth around me, and I came like that, watching him and wondering how I'd gotten so goddamn lucky.

He let me slip out of his mouth, careful with me, with how sensitive I'd be. I tugged at his arms, urging him toward me, and between the two of us, we got his jeans open so I could take him in my hand. I stroked up and down while I got my breath back from the orgasm. He didn't seem like he'd mind if that was all that happened, but I wanted my mouth on him, his taste on my lips. I brought my knees up and pulled him forward so he was right there, and I took him in.

It didn't take him very long. I wished it had lasted, actually, but there'd be time for that later, when we weren't sitting under a tree.

He kissed me right after, which was maybe the hottest thing that had happened to me, ever.

After, we slumped together under the tree, my arms around him, and just breathed. Our clothes were still all over the place—I was mostly naked, and I was pretty sure that my fears about what I might sit on were well founded. I thought there was a stick poking me in the ass—but we took a second to come down.

I pushed his hair off his forehead and kissed him. "That was . . . intense."

He laughed softly. "Yeah. I needed that. Thanks."

He slipped an arm around my waist, and even though I knew we should be getting up and going, knew that someone could find us here any minute, I held him tighter. Just for a while, I thought, we could sit here and be with each other, alone. I felt him smile into my skin when I brushed my fingers through his hair.

"You're in a good mood." I kept my voice low.

He shrugged. "You're here, we're playing shows. I love being on tour. What's not to be happy about?"

I took a breath. I was starting to get chilly, lying here without anything on, but I didn't want to move yet. "Sometimes you look . . . so tired." I didn't really want to talk about this, not now. But his words made me curious. "Sometimes I wondered if you didn't like touring."

He shook his head. "I love touring. It's the best part of making music. It's the part when you know you've done what you needed to do, wrote the songs the best you could, put them out there, and people liked them. It's all the vanity and pride of being a rock star, all wrapped up together." He sighed. "But it's . . . a lot, you know? A lot of going and going. A lot of people taking and taking."

"They give back too," I said, thinking about how I loved being in a crowd for a concert, how much I wanted to show the band that I was thrilled they were there, that I considered myself lucky to be able to see them play.

"They definitely do," he said quickly. "That's why I love it. There isn't anything better than that."

We sat for a while longer, and then it really did get too cold, and we had to get up. He brushed grass off me, and I picked a leaf out of his hair, and he actually giggled. It made me feel like we'd gotten away with something. Together. I caught his hand while we walked back, and he swung our hands between us.

"The next date, in Dallas? That's where I grew up. Or right outside of it."

"Okay." I'd been vaguely aware that Bellamy had grown up somewhere near there, but I hadn't been exactly sure. He'd moved to California when he'd been barely out of high school, as far as I knew. He'd thought it'd be easier to find a band there, and sure enough, he'd met Ava and Tuck while they'd been going to college.

He was staring straight ahead and didn't meet my eyes as he spoke. "I really . . . I don't like it there," he said simply, but it didn't sound simple at all. It sounded like there was a whole world of bad memories and emotions tucked behind those words. "I don't like going back. But Dallas likes to claim me as its homegrown musician, and the scene is pretty good, actually, so we always do."

"Bellamy . . ."

He turned to me then, stopping us right there in the path, before we got to the gate that would take us to the parking lot and the bus. "I'm telling you this because, when we're there, I'm not . . . myself. And everybody else knows to just leave me alone, but you won't. There's no reason you'd know. So I'm telling you now so you do."

I shook my head and laughed. "I'm not leaving you alone." Then I thought about how nearly stalkerish that sounded. "Do you want me to leave you alone?"

He shrugged, and the movement pulled on our joined hands. "I don't know. I just know I'm not great to be around."

I squeezed his fingers. "Let's just see how it goes, okay?" If he knew the place made him unhappy, I figured that was half the battle right there. And I could admit that I thought he was being a tiny bit dramatic. I'd seen him when he was unhappy, when he was doing his best to write because he had to and it was bringing him down. He hadn't been exactly cheery, but it hadn't been anything that had made me want to stay away from him, either. "Don't push me away yet. All right?"

He nodded, and I thought he looked almost hopeful. Like I'd given him something fragile he wanted to hold on to. We walked back to the bus, and we didn't talk about it again.

chapter ten

bellamy seemed really buoyant over the next day as we meandered our way up the east side of Texas, enough that I figured he really had been putting too much thought into how he'd be when we got back to his hometown. Maybe he was simply nervous. I mostly put it out of my head, because it didn't seem important.

The day we arrived in Dallas, Bellamy withdrew a bit, but I figured that was normal too. We holed up in his bunk—he read and I sketched, and it was quiet but not uncomfortable at all. That afternoon, after we'd set up and Escaping Indigo had done sound check, they had an acoustic gig at a local record store. Ava was only taking a cajón, a box-like, all-in-one drum that I was seriously coveting, so I didn't have to go with them. I was roadie-duty-free for the rest of the evening, until the band went on.

By the time they got back, Bellamy was even quieter. He seemed as if he'd gone inward, as if he was concentrating hard on something, or as if he was storing up energy.

When he got on stage, though, he seemed . . . perfect. More than fine. Electric and lit up from the inside. He threw everything he had into that performance. He did that every night, but this time, it seemed like he was trying even harder, was giving that tiny bit more, was pushing himself to the edge.

The audience loved it. They fed on his energy, took and took and took. Any other night, I would have been thrilled to see the excitement, the joy, on their faces. That night, though, I was almost afraid. It was like Bellamy was giving away parts of himself, and I wasn't sure what he'd have left when the night was over. All I could do was stand there and watch him, though: watch his spine bend with the music, watch his body curve around the guitar, watch the strain in his arms when he raised them above his head. Stand there and adore him, like I'd been adoring him for years, admiring him, wishing I could see the world like he did, through this layer of sound and noise and words and tangible energy, art made solid.

In the middle of the show, he stopped and told the audience about how he'd grown up right here, how this venue had been the one he'd gone to to see bands play. He made it sound nostalgic, but I'd gotten pretty good at seeing the tight lines of tension in his shoulders, the way he kept one hand tucked into his pocket when he was stressed, and I saw that while he chatted up the audience. He spoke well, though. I wondered if there were kids like him and me and Eric in the audience, people who only wanted a connection, wanted to know that this place and the feelings of being different or outcast didn't last forever. Bellamy gave that to people, simply by getting up on stage and making music like he did.

Bellamy headed straight to the bus after the show. That wasn't unusual either. Quinn and I took our time taking the gear off the stage, and Ava came and helped us pull the drum set apart and put it into cases.

When we were done, I went for a smoke, half expecting to find Bellamy. He wasn't there, though. I finished and came back, to find Tuck leaning against the side of the bus. He had a cigarette between his fingers, but he wasn't smoking it. The ash was so long I figured he'd forgotten about it. He glanced up when he noticed me, and gave me a tired smile. "Bellamy's in the back."

I shoved my hands in my pockets. "He was . . . He was on fire, on stage."

"Yeah." He waved his hand, and the ash fell off his cigarette. He stared at it, then at his hand, like he was surprised to find the cigarette wedged between his fingers. "It was a good show. Glad it's done, though. Bellamy's better when we're not here."

I nodded. Tuck jerked his head at the bus. He fished around in his pocket for another cigarette, and I turned and went up the bus stairs. It was quiet inside. Ava and Quinn were nowhere to be seen. Lissa sat on the couch near the door. She gave me a shy smile, and I returned it, but she didn't say anything. I liked that about Lissa, that she was so comfortable being silent.

I moved toward the back of the bus, pausing to pull aside the corner of the curtain that covered Bellamy's bunk. It was empty. I pushed aside the next curtain and stepped into the back room. Bellamy was sitting on the floor, his back against the couch. He had his hand on a guitar, like he'd been plucking at the strings, but he was still now. I paused, not really sure what I should do. He probably wanted space. But I didn't want to leave him here alone. I didn't want him to not have the option of being with someone, if that was what he wanted.

I moved around a guitar case, open on the floor, and sat on the couch, far enough away that we didn't quite touch. I could feel the heat of his shoulder through my jeans, though.

"Hey." I was the king of witty openers.

"Hey." He glanced up at me and gave me a tiny smile.

"You okay?"

He nodded and tilted his head back so he could look up at me. "Yup. Tired. I just hate this city. And I hate that the tour's almost over. And I'm . . . tired."

"Yeah." I shifted, bumping his elbow with my knee. "Well, I . . ."

"I always feel better after I play. On stage or not." He certainly sounded tired. His voice was thin, ragged from singing and soft enough that I could hear the exhaustion in it. He tipped to the side and leaned his head against the knee that I'd brushed him with. "You were right about that, before."

"Yeah." I always felt better when I pounded away on a drum set. Maybe it was a bit different, the exertion and the release, but I didn't think it could be that far off. It was less about the exercise, the push and pull of muscles, and more about the music and what I let it leach out of me.

"They think we're fearless," he mumbled into the fabric of my jeans.

I hesitated, then dropped my hand and stroked his hair back from his face. "Who?"

"The fans. They think we're fearless. They think that's why we can do what we do. Stand in front of people, put ourselves out there.

Sing. Make music." He took a deep breath, let it out of him in a slow whoosh. His hand had settled on my ankle, and he tightened his fingers, a tiny bit. "We're not. We just hide it better."

There was a certain bravery in it. I knew that. It took something you didn't know you had inside you to get up there on stage, to put the music you made out there for people to listen to. Or, at least, it always had for me.

I nodded. He wasn't watching me, couldn't see the movement, but I thought maybe the quiet was enough of an answer anyway. We sat like that, his hand on me and my fingers in his hair, for a minute longer.

"Do you want me to go?" I asked softly. He'd gotten heavy against me, and I wasn't sure if he was falling asleep. It was fine with me if he wanted to, even though we'd both end up with sore joints from sitting like this. But I wondered too if maybe he wanted to be alone and I'd interrupted.

He pushed himself up a little, but he didn't move away. "Not really."

The curtain at the front of the room pulled back, and Tuck stuck his head around it. I glanced up at him and caught his eyes. He was staring at us, and he blinked at me and shrugged, asking me without words if we were okay. I didn't know if we were. I didn't know if Bellamy was all right. But I didn't think he *wasn't* all right, either. He was worn out and emotionally drained, and it made me nervous, but I thought I could handle it.

I nodded at Tuck, and after a second, he backed up and let the curtain fall into place.

"You're not going to try to make me happy right now, are you?" Bellamy asked, his words floating up between us.

I almost laughed. "No, sweetheart." I ran my fingers through his hair again, letting them tangle in the strands at his neck. "I'd be terrible at that."

He did laugh, the sound surprised and sharp. "How freaked-out about this are you?"

My hand stilled, and I had to focus to keep stroking it through his hair. "I'm not," I said, but it was almost a lie. I *was* freaked-out. This wasn't Bellamy bemoaning that he couldn't think up anything to write. This wasn't Bellamy feeling slightly down. This was . . . such a small thing, and it looked like it was crushing him. He looked trampled on, like he'd have to claw his way back to being happy, and seeing that on him was frightening. I didn't like it. That strain didn't belong on Bellamy's face.

Bellamy didn't reply to that. He sighed again, his breath gusting over my knee. "Should we get up and go to bed?" He didn't make a move to go anywhere, didn't even lift his hand off my foot.

"In a minute," I said. "We can sit here some more, if you want."

"I do." So we did, until my knee started to freeze up and he said he was getting a crick in his neck. Then we stood together and moved to the bunks, and right before he disappeared into the bathroom, I felt his hand run from my elbow to my fingers, a long, slow touch. He leaned over and kissed my cheek, and I squeezed my fingers around his once before we let go.

chapter eleven

X

i wanted to see Bellamy the next morning, but the first people I ran into were Tuck and Lissa. They were in the back room, piled on each other on the couch while they had their coffee. I started to leave, to give them some privacy in case they wanted a few minutes alone, but Tuck waved to me and invited me to sit.

I hadn't spent too much time with either of them. I made sure all of Tuck's guitars were tuned and ready for him, and sometimes I helped Lissa carry in boxes of merch for each show, but most of my time had been spent with Quinn and Ava. And Bellamy. Tuck and Lissa seemed like cool people. I just didn't really know them.

Tuck made things pretty simple by keeping it on a subject we could both relate to. "Thanks for hanging out with Bellamy last night."

I raised my eyebrows. "Sure. Does someone . . . usually hang out with him?"

He shrugged. "He likes to be by himself when he's feeling low, actually. Most times, he won't let anyone be with him. I think it was good for him, though. That you were there."

Lissa nodded. She'd had her legs swung over Tuck's lap, but when I came in, she'd sat up, tucking her legs under her. "He needs somebody."

I sighed. I wished I'd gotten my own cup of coffee before I'd come in. I needed something to do with my hands. "I've never seen him like that before."

Tuck raised his eyebrows. "I'm not gonna say it's exactly normal, but . . . Bellamy has his moments."

Lissa cleared her throat. "Umm, Micah, did Bellamy . . . tell you anything?"

I nodded. I liked that she wanted to talk about this, but wanted to protect Bellamy's privacy at the same time. "Yeah. We talked about his anxiety. I just . . . I've never really seen it in action, I guess." Or that wasn't quite right. I *had* seen it. But some of that time, I hadn't known what it was. And it had never been like it was last night. "I've never seen it like that. It wasn't ever . . . that bad."

She nodded. Tuck rubbed his hand over her knee. She smiled up at him, more comfortable and easy than I'd ever seen her. She looked at him like she could have a whole conversation with him without saying a word. I got the feeling they looked at each other like that an awful lot.

"He doesn't like to talk about it," Tuck said, turning back to me. "But I think it's a good sign that he told you."

"But you know about it," I said. It wasn't a dig. It was more an observation, and a hint at wanting more information, if they wanted to give it.

He shrugged again. He seemed pretty easy with the whole conversation, but I wondered if he was remembering Bellamy's last boyfriend too, and how badly that seemed to have gone. The band had only been good to me, open and friendly. They'd let me into their space and treated me like I wasn't just the new guy. But I *was* the new guy. They'd known each other for years—even Lissa had been with them longer than I had. I was the unknown.

He and Lissa exchanged another glance. She covered his hand with hers on her knee.

"I think," Tuck said, slow, "people think about anxiety like this . . . cute little quirk. Like some minor social annoyance that people have. And I'm not saying that some people don't have it like that. Fuck, man, I don't really know anything about it. But I know that with Bellamy, it isn't . . . small like that. It's a big thing. Sometimes it's gone and he's fine and you'd never know at all. And sometimes something so tiny sets him off and he sinks into it, and it's like he can't figure out what move to make at all. It becomes something else. It traps him. It's scary and it's debilitating."

It *was* scary. I could feel myself drawing back, like I was trying to pull away from the conversation. When I realized what I was doing, I made myself lean forward again. "Does he . . . do anything about it?"

Lissa stared down at her lap. "He handles it."

Tuck nodded in agreement. "He always does."

"Yeah, but . . . does he see anyone? A doctor? Does he take anything for it?" Anxiety drugs were a thing. Weren't they?

Tuck was shaking his head before I even finished talking. "He doesn't want to."

I blinked. That seemed . . . sort of ridiculous. "Why not?"

Tuck just shook his head again, and that was pretty much the end of that conversation. Lissa started talking about a book she was reading that Tuck had given her, and it turned out I'd read it a few months ago. We got so involved in discussing the characters that I forgot for a few minutes that I had anything else to worry about.

I did bring it up with Bellamy later, though. We'd stopped for the night in a rest area—we were between shows, and everyone had seemed glad to head to their own corners of the bus and, as much as we all could, have some time to ourselves. Bellamy and I had scrunched up together on the couch in the back room. Quinn had sat in the nearby chair for a while, but when it got late, he retreated to his bunk. It was only me and Bellamy, the bus quiet around us, and dark, lit only by the security lights in the parking lot of the rest area.

"Do you want to talk about last night?" I kept my voice low.

He snuggled closer to me. He had a book in his hands, but he hadn't been reading it for a while. He'd been staring off into space. I thought he might have been writing in his mind, working out lyrics or melodies. He'd do that sometimes—sit and stare for a long while, then grab a guitar and have most of a song worked out.

"No." He let the book drop. "Do you?"

I did. I really did. But I didn't know where to start, and I didn't think it was fair to make him talk about it because *I* wanted to.

"I just . . . wanted to make sure you were okay."

He didn't quite cross his arms, but he looked like he wanted to. As if he wanted to draw himself in, keep himself to himself. I thought of the first day we'd met, the first day we'd started working together. Quinn had introduced us, and Bellamy had kept his arms tucked tight against his sides, hands in his pockets. A position casual enough that it wouldn't make anyone look twice, but defensive. Like he was holding himself in. Or holding me out.

"I'm fine," he said.

"Bellamy . . ."

"Micah." He unfolded a bit, twisting so he could see me. His chin rested on my chest. "You could still be a drummer."

I blinked at the change in subject. "I know."

"It would be hard, but you could do it."

I drew in a breath, let it out slow. "It's not about how hard it would be. It's about . . . knowing what I'm capable of."

He blinked. The streetlight was highlighting his cheek in orange, showing off the sharp curve of his jaw, his long nose. His hair was every which way, tangled and falling in his face. He was wild and lovely and worn. And human. More human than I thought I'd ever seen him.

He reached out, almost tentative, and touched his fingertip to my arm, let it coast down to my wrist. "You're a great drummer."

"Thanks." I felt myself blushing with the easy praise, shivering at his touch. I tried to concentrate. "But you don't actually know that." I shook my head. "It's not about that, either. Not about how good I am, I mean. It's how much I'm willing to work for it. How badly I want it."

"You wanted it when Eric was alive."

I nodded. "Yeah."

He shifted again, so he was sitting up next to me. His legs were still pressed against me. He let his head flop back against the couch cushion. He looked sleepy. I wanted to take him back to a bunk, his or mine, and curl up around him, just hold him for a while. I wondered if it'd be weird if we slept on the couch together. There was more room out here.

"But now you don't want that."

"I don't know, Bellamy. I don't know what I want."

"You missed your shot."

"Yeah."

"You really think that?" His voice wasn't much more than a breath. We were so close now. His face was a couple of inches from mine, if that. We were breathing the same air, and it wouldn't take more than a fraction of movement to bring us together, to bring his lips to mine, to let us move in toward each other.

I wanted it. I wanted to do it and stop this conversation. "Why are we talking about this? We were talking about you."

I raised my head and met his eyes, and he grinned. "Because I don't want to talk about me. I want to know . . . I want to know why you're here. Not *here*." He gestured broadly, like he was taking in the parking lot and the bus. "But with us."

A sigh escaped me. "Then, yes. Most of the time, I really think that. That I missed my shot."

"And the rest?"

I wondered if I'd ever get used to his voice, aimed at me. I wondered if there'd ever be a time when I'd heard it so often that I didn't automatically want to answer his every question, do whatever he asked of me.

I shook my head. I was afraid of what I'd say. That I'd tell him that sometimes I missed it so much it was like a hole inside me, a hollow space I couldn't fill. That sometimes I wanted it so badly I could taste it, could feel it on me like a second skin. That I was never sure if I was doing the right thing, making the right choices.

"Being in a band . . . I don't think I'm built for that," I told him. "Not without Eric."

He nodded. "Okay."

"That's it?"

He ducked his head, his hair making a red-gold halo around his face. "You want me to say something else?"

"No." I shook my head. "I'm just surprised it was that easy to convince you."

He smiled at me again, a tiny lift in his mouth. "I've had people tell me my whole life what I should or shouldn't do. Most of the time, I'm still the only one who knows what I want." He brushed his thumb over my knuckles, then pulled his hand away. "I make my own choices. You make yours. That's fair."

I swallowed. "If you make your own choices, then why aren't you getting any help for this anxiety you have?"

He laughed. "What would I say to someone? I have this thing that isn't exactly a problem, and isn't super visible? Or, maybe, I have the job most people on the planet would trade their souls for, and I love it, but it makes me stressed? That's ridiculous." He hadn't raised his voice, but he definitely sounded angry, or like he might almost be angry. I wondered if he'd tried to explain this to people before, or if he'd kept it close and secret.

"I think it's kind of a problem," I said softly. "If it hurts you, it's a problem."

He shrugged, but his shoulders were tight and he was angling them in like he was trying to protect himself. "If I tell someone, they're just . . . going to tell me to suck it up or stop being so dramatic. That's what people always say. Because I'm never quite dramatic enough, never enough that anyone thinks something's wrong."

I thought that was unfair, almost cruel, to himself and to everyone who did show their issues that way. But I didn't say anything. I let him keep going.

"No one wants to believe a rock star when he tells them he's depressed or anxious. I have the perfect life, you know? Why would I be depressed? It's just . . . a quiet thing that happens. I can handle it. I always have before."

"But . . ." I shook my head. "Someone might be able to help you. If you could talk to someone, or take something . . ." A shocked expression came over his face, and I trailed off.

"I don't want to take anything. What if I can't stop? What if I use it as a crutch and then I can't ever go without? I don't want to start using something and let it take control of me. I want to be myself."

It sounded like he'd actually thought about this, and I wanted to respect that. But I still thought that maybe, at least a little, he was letting the fear of what he didn't know sway him. "It's not the same. I don't think it's like that." But I was hesitant because, the fact was, I didn't know how it was. I didn't know what drugs they gave someone like Bellamy, and I didn't know what they'd do. "Is that something you're seriously afraid of?"

He hesitated, then nodded.

"You could say that to whoever you talk to. You could . . . You could try different things."

"You're not hearing me." His voice went hard. "I don't want to."

"Because you're afraid," I pressed.

"Because it's my choice!"

I threw my hands up. "Well, what kind of choice is it when this . . . thing decides who you can be, and who you can be with, for you?"

It was the wrong thing to say, and I knew it as soon as I said it. I reached out for him, but I didn't know if he'd let me touch him, so my hands hovered awkwardly between us. "I'm sorry." My voice came out on a sharp breath. "I'm so sorry. I didn't mean that."

For a second, he didn't say anything, and I was afraid, so afraid, that I'd ruined this already, let my mouth run off and said something I didn't mean, and he'd see I wasn't worth the trouble after all. Then he looked down. His bangs fell in his eyes, and I couldn't see his expression.

"You're right. It rules me. When I'm in the middle of it, it owns me."

I covered his hand with mine. I was afraid he'd pull away, but he didn't. "Bellamy, I didn't mean that. I don't think it rules you. I think you do your very best to control it and protect people from it. Protect yourself. And I know you're afraid, but . . ." I thought of him up on the stage, night after night, good nights and bad nights, when he wasn't feeling it and when he was. How he always gave just as much of himself, how he never held anything back. "I also think you're one of the bravest people I know." It was a silly thing to say, but I felt it, and I wanted him to know. "But I hate to see you hurting. And yesterday . . . I was scared. I didn't know how to help."

He sighed and leaned forward to rest his head on my shoulder. "I know. I'm sorry too. But you know you can't fix it, right?" He pulled back again just as suddenly, catching my eye. "If you start trying to fix it . . . Because it can't be fixed, Micah. There's no fix. Just a Band-Aid that someone will try to slap on it. I don't want that."

I nodded, even though I wasn't one hundred percent convinced of that. People got help for this. Didn't they? Maybe this was different. Maybe Bellamy was right—it wasn't as if I had any experience with this. I didn't know anything about it. And Bellamy had, like he'd said, been living with it all this time. It just seemed wrong that nothing could be done. I couldn't stop thinking about Eric. About how, if Eric had gotten some help, things might have turned out differently. If he'd opened up and told us, if he'd let us find him someone to talk to . . . But Bellamy wasn't Eric. I'd said as much to Quinn the other day.

"Okay." I moved my hand away from his, then held out my arm, nervous and hoping he'd take the invitation. He curled up against me, and I breathed a sigh of relief. "Okay. I'm sorry."

"Don't be sorry," he said, soft, into the fabric of my T-shirt.

I let out a tiny laugh. "I want to be careful with you. I want to make you happy. I don't want you to realize . . ." I trailed off, embarrassed. He made me want to tell him everything, to be open with everything I was feeling.

"Realize what?" he asked.

I shook my head. I didn't want him to realize that I was only the roadie. That he was a rock star—maybe not the most famous rock star ever, or the biggest, but a star nonetheless, and someone I had always admired—and he could have anyone he wanted instead of me. I didn't want him to realize how small I was in comparison to him. But I definitely didn't want to blurt any of that out.

"I just don't want to screw this up," I admitted instead.

He tilted his face up and kissed the side of my jaw. "You won't." I felt him smile against my skin. "You called me sweetheart."

"Huh?"

"Last night." He tucked his face against the curve of my neck, and his words came out all muffled and warm. "You called me sweetheart."

"Oh." My face heated, and I knew my cheeks were probably going deep red with a blush. I remembered saying the endearment, but I hadn't thought much about it then. It had just popped out, like every other damn thing that spilled out of my mouth unchecked when Bellamy was around. "Sorry."

He took my hand and flexed his fingers against mine. "I liked it."

"Yeah?" I tried to find any teasing in his voice, but I didn't think he was. I tightened my arm around him.

"Yeah."

I hesitated, and then sighed. "Good."

"You gonna do it again?"

My lungs felt too tight. "Maybe."

Another smile. I couldn't see it, but I didn't have to. "I hope you do."

The warmth that gave me stayed with me until we went to bed, squashed into one bunk, Bellamy wrapped around me, our heads sharing the same pillow. I woke up the next morning with a crick in my neck and my legs cramped from being jammed into the small space, but I couldn't work up any annoyance about it at all.

X

Bellamy was himself over the next week, and he . . . wasn't. He seemed happy most of the time, and really into the shows we played in Denver, Tempe, and Tucson. He had favorite restaurants in each place—an Indian place in a strip mall in Denver, a Mexican place in Tempe that we had to get a cab for, and a Thai place in Tucson that made the best bubble tea I'd ever had. He seemed downright giddy to show me these places, to show off the cities like they were his home, and I thought, in a way, that maybe they were. He lived in San Diego, with the rest of the band, but maybe his home was on the road. Maybe he felt that the place where he belonged was with the road stretched out in front of him, and concerts for him to play, night after night after night.

If I hadn't been looking, if I hadn't thought I was getting to know him, I might not have seen anything at all that felt off. But I was looking, and the closer we got to home, the more he seemed to draw into himself. He was just . . . quiet. It wasn't even anything I could really pinpoint, except that it was like he was pulling away from me, and I didn't understand what was happening.

When we crossed the state line into California, it was like he sensed it. Aside from the show in Dallas, Bellamy had been fine. But now he retreated to his bunk with a book, and he kept his curtain partially closed. If someone talked to him, he answered and seemed fine, but he didn't seek anyone out, and everyone kept their distance.

I kept my distance for a while too. I didn't want to be clingy or needy. But I *was* clingy and needy, probably more so than normal. I'd had people slip away from me. I didn't want to let it happen again. So that afternoon I scratched my fingernails down his curtain, a gentle knocking, and when he pulled it back, I asked if I could sit with him.

He scooted backward and drew his legs in, and I sat across from him. He pulled the curtain closed again, so we were in our own small, warm, dark space, and it was almost as if we were alone.

"Do you hate California?" I asked, because I didn't know, really, how to start the conversation, or even exactly what conversation I wanted to have. That was just what popped out when I opened my mouth.

It made him laugh. "No. I love it here."

I smiled back. "You don't seem to."

He shrugged and set his book aside. "I like touring. It's been . . ." He rocked his head back and forth. "A bit harder, this time. Because I was with my boyfriend last time, and I kept remembering, and . . . everything's been weird since we broke up. For me."

I wanted to remind him that I was here instead. I wanted to make up for the feelings he was missing. But I knew he didn't mean it like that, and I knew feelings of loss didn't work that way, so I nodded, even though I couldn't help being a tiny bit jealous.

"I don't hate California, though. I like being home. I just like touring better. Usually touring's when I'm . . . happiest, really. When I feel like myself the most."

"But not this time."

He shook his head. "This time I was low."

"And now . . ." I was trying to understand. Touring *was* fun. But it was exhausting too. I was glad to only do it in limited pieces. I would never have wanted to go on and on, stuck on the bus, stuck with the same people, even when they were people I really liked. Stuck watching the scenery and the cities pass us by in an endless blur. I was happy to have been on tour, and I'd be happy when we got to go home and I could shower in my own bathroom.

"Now it's the end of the tour, and I . . . I never know . . . what to do, how to be, when we're not on the road. And we have to write a new album, and I like that, I do." He glanced up at me, then back down, to his hands folded in his lap. "But it makes me nervous. What if it's not good enough? What if the magic doesn't work this time? What if we don't try hard enough?" He shook his head. "I know that's weird."

"It's not." I understood fear, and this was a fragile business. People always assumed that once you made it, got a record deal or went on tour, you were a superstar. But you were still just like everyone else— scrambling to make it in a tough world. And there were always things that could fall apart, especially when you were relying on so many other people, especially when you were relying so much on your own ability to be creative. I saw Bellamy and the rest of the band as this huge force, but when it came down to it, they were just people who wanted to keep doing the thing that they loved.

"Can I help?" I asked. He started to shake his head, but I didn't want him to just push me aside, to assume I didn't understand. Maybe it wasn't all clear, but I wasn't an idiot, either. "Maybe . . . maybe if you talked to the band about it more, instead of hiding out . . ." I let my voice trail off. He was watching me, but in the gloom of the bunk I couldn't quite read his expression. "Maybe if, when we get home, you could see someone. A therapist or something? I know you don't think it'll help, but I think it might."

"I told you I didn't want to do that. I told you how I felt about that." His voice was low and he sounded confused, wary, and it made me want to do something to make him feel better even more. "Why are you so stuck on this? Why do you keep coming back to it?"

"Because I don't know how to help," I said. "And I hate seeing you hurting, and I want to do something—"

"But I don't want you to do anything!"

I definitely didn't need to guess at what he was feeling there. The confusion had gone, and he only sounded angry.

"Look," I pressed, searching for a way to make this better. I didn't want him angry at me. It erased the times when we'd been so close and he'd been so human, made me go right back to those moments when he was Bellamy and I was the roadie, wasn't his equal. It made me feel so small. "I know you're nervous because of what happened with your last boyfriend, but I'm not him. I can take it. I can do better, I promise. I just want to help, I want to find an answer for you, I want to fix what's hurting you . . ."

He raised his hands like he was trying to ward me off, and I shut my mouth. "I don't want that, don't you get it? I don't want you to fix anything because you *can't*. And if you start trying, you'll only be disappointed with me, and you'll leave."

I shook my head, trying to talk over him. "No, I won't, Bellamy. When Eric was down, I—"

"I'm not Eric," he said, sharp and hard. "You keep telling me you're not my ex. Well, I'm not Eric. I don't want you to fix me. I don't want you to . . ." He spread his hands. "I don't even know. Fill a hole inside me? I know it doesn't work like that." He poked a finger at me. "You're so gung-ho about me getting counseling. Have you thought maybe that's what you need? Some help so you're not seeing him every damn place you look? So you don't see him in me?"

To have something that I had intended to be helpful and good thrown back at me stung. And to have him make it about Eric felt like a much worse attack. It mixed with what Quinn had said, about not confusing Eric and Bellamy, and tangled up in my head until it was all hurt and anger and loss and confusion, and I didn't know how to untangle it or deal with it or address it. I breathed in, but it didn't feel like anything happened. No air. No nothing. I was sinking. I tried to swallow, and my throat was bone dry.

"You're wrong. I don't . . ." I couldn't make anything add up in my head, let alone get out a coherent sentence. I couldn't figure out how we'd gone from sitting together and talking to arguing so vilely. I couldn't figure out how I'd gone from being fast on my way to loving him, to being so angry I wanted to reach across the space between us and slap him. Show him, somehow, how much it hurt for him to say those things. "I don't think that, I don't think you're . . . You're wrong. You don't know him. You don't know."

He nodded. He was so pale, the blood leached out of his skin. His jaw was clamped so tight I could see the muscles working. "I know you're so wrapped up in him you've stopped doing what you love. I know you could be in a band if you wanted, but you're here instead, working for us, because you can't let him go."

He sounded so gentle, even though I knew he was angry. But instead of making me want to listen to what he was saying, it only made me ache inside, in a way I hadn't thought I could ache. Like my heart was breaking for Eric all over again because Bellamy was saying these things. And it was worse because it *was* Bellamy saying it, Bellamy who I cared about.

I pushed away from him, shoved the curtain back, and climbed out of the bunk so I could get a tiny bit of space between us. "We're back to that again. All you care about is whether I'm in a band or not. You don't care about how I feel, or how I feel about you." I breathed out and tried to be rational, logical, but I couldn't. There wasn't any moment between what I was thinking and what I was saying, no time for me to filter anything or think about what the consequences might be.

"You want to know why I'm so stuck on this, Bellamy?" I asked. "Maybe it is because of Eric. Because I saw him in pain and I saw him lose control, and I don't want that to happen to you. Maybe it's because I believe you when you tell me that this thing inside you is serious. Or maybe it's because I care about you, so I want to help you, and I can't." I swallowed. My throat was so dry I wanted to cough, but I couldn't stop ranting at him yet. He stared up at me, his eyes wide, his pupils huge in the dark. "I know you'd stand by me if I was hurting. If I was down. I don't have to question that, I just know. And I want to do the same, but I *don't know what to do.*" I flicked my hand, like I was flicking it all away. Like it was a simple thing, even though it so obviously wasn't. "That's why. That's the only way it has anything to do with Eric. I didn't want him to hurt. And I feel the same about you. But you don't care about that. You just want to protect yourself."

His mouth dropped open, but nothing came out. He raised his hands, and I couldn't tell if he was going to plead with me or push me away. I wasn't sure he knew. He didn't look nearly as angry anymore. He looked confused.

Made sense to me. That was how I felt too.

He was looking at me, and I didn't know what he saw. The man he'd been slipping into a relationship with? The guy he'd been sleeping with? Did he see me as his equal? Or was I always going to be the roadie to him, always someone who couldn't understand how he was feeling, what his life was like? As soon as I had the thought, I didn't want to know. I'd said too much, and so had he. I wasn't sure I wanted him to try to say anything else, either, because right then I didn't want to hear it. I was already hurting too much. There was a tiny voice in the back of my mind that was saying that I had maybe tried to hurt him just as much.

"Micah."

I thought he was going to reach for me. I took a step back and shook my head. He dropped his hand, and shrank back against the bunk's wall.

I knew leaving things like this was the wrong thing to do, but I didn't know what the right thing was, and my brain wasn't about to come up with the answer while I was so tangled in all of this. I turned and climbed into my bunk, and pulled the curtain shut behind me. I heard Bellamy's footsteps moving down the hallway a few minutes later. I thought he paused outside my bunk, but he didn't pull back the curtain, and he didn't say anything.

chapter twelve

i thought Bellamy and I would talk, but over the last few days of the tour, he managed to avoid me completely. It would have been a neat trick, in such an enclosed space, at any other time. But now it only made the ache in me hurt more.

On the other hand, I didn't seek him out, either. I was still angry, and every time I thought about what he'd said, it hurt all over again and made me even more frustrated.

We finished out the last couple of dates in Los Angeles and finally in San Diego, and then we were home. It was strange. When we'd first gone out on the road, being stuck on the bus had made the hours and days crawl by so slowly. After a while, though, I couldn't imagine not being there. And now I couldn't imagine being in the same city for more than a couple of days at a time. I couldn't imagine being home.

I spent the first week home missing everyone from the band. When I was on the bus, sometimes I'd thought I'd scream just for wanting, so badly, to have a little privacy, a little time to myself where I couldn't hear at least two other people talking. But now that I was alone, it felt like I was too alone. I missed the quiet chatter and the soft sounds of a guitar, or Ava thumping away with her sticks on a practice pad, or the pings and buzzes of a video game. Bellamy's laughter at Lissa's dry sense of humor. The drone of the bus engine, the shushing of wheels over tarmac.

My apartment above Eric's mother's garage was too still, too empty. I'd always liked how big it was, how there weren't many walls, so all the rooms seeped into each other, the kitchen into the living room into the bedroom. I liked the way the light came in through the big windows that lined one wall. The breeze that came through those windows, smelling of city and diesel but also of the backyard lawn, the sharp green of fresh-cut grass. But even the noise from the street, the hum of conversations and traffic passing by, the knowledge that Eric's mother was only a short walk across the driveway, didn't quite keep the silence and the loneliness away.

The apartment felt like home too, though. That was almost stranger than the sudden quiet. I'd lived there since I was eighteen, and Eric had lived with me sometimes too. The place had always been more mine than his. But it still seemed like I could feel him there, or feel the absence of him, in the way the air moved around me, the creak of the floors and the stillness of the room when I was getting ready to go to bed. Sometimes, when I lay still, I imagined I could hear him, see him out of the corner of my eye. I missed him so much that I always hoped I was right, that he was somewhere near, that if I turned my head just right, I'd see him. But I knew I wouldn't, that he wasn't some ghost haunting me. It was only memories and hopes, and the possibilities they taunted me with hurt almost as much as the missing him did.

And I missed Bellamy. I didn't want to. I wanted to be angry with him, hurt enough that I didn't want to see him. I was angry, even though I was sometimes sure the argument and how wrong it had all gone was my fault. It wasn't enough to stop me from wanting to see him, though. To wish that maybe things had turned out differently. Bellamy and the rest of the band didn't live very far away at all, but it felt like they might as well have been on the other side of the world. Bellamy was once again unattainable, a fantasy that I had seen through, to his true self, but still craved.

Escaping Indigo had a last few festival dates, later in the summer. I was contracted to work them, and since no one had fired me yet, I assumed I still would. Until then, I planned to waste away the last of the long, hot summer days. I read and listened to music, and I drew. I drew things from memory, and I drew things I saw: still lifes of my coffeepot, the way the covers on the bed rucked up at the end, the heat coming off the street. I drew the band, trying to imagine their faces in my mind, get their features just right. Ava at the drum set, Tuck on stage, a guitar cradled in his hands. And Bellamy. Bellamy singing and

Bellamy asleep and Bellamy sitting in the back room, playing guitar when he thought no one was watching.

And I played drums. For a long time after Eric died, after I'd finally picked up the sticks again, playing had simply been something I'd done because practice had always been mandatory in my mind. If I didn't play at least once in a while, I'd lose my touch. There wasn't a reason for me to keep my touch anymore, really, but it had tied into my brain with the things Quinn had said to me, when he saw how I was sleeping away my days. Playing kept me grounded, gave me a routine, gave me something to focus on, so I didn't slip back into missing Eric with such a single-mindedness that I wanted to join him.

Now, though, it was different. The first time I sat behind the kit after we got home, I felt it. Some kind of freedom that ran through my hands and my feet. I had told Bellamy that I didn't want to be a drummer in a band that was trying to make it anymore. I'd meant it too. But somewhere along the tour, watching Escaping Indigo, watching Ava, missing Eric, missing being on a stage, being part of that, it had settled in me, going from a vague notion of what I didn't want into a certainty. I didn't know what it was I *did* want. But it wasn't this.

The thing was, even before Eric died, drumming had not been, for a while, what I thought it should be. I couldn't remember when the last time was that I hadn't thought of it as a job. Strictly as a job. As a means to an end. Since I'd played because I wanted to, because it made me feel good, instead of because I had to. Drumming did center me. But it wasn't *central* to me. I thought that if it were central, like writing songs was to Bellamy, like music had been to Eric, like drumming was for Ava, I would always feel that. Maybe sometimes it would be further away. But I would always feel like it was a part of me, the largest part of me. And . . . I didn't. It wasn't. I wasn't sure if it ever had been, or if I'd only hoped that it would be.

I thought about Ava, about when I watched her play. She sat at the kit and moved her body over the drums and the cymbals and the pedals like they were part of her. Like she knew every single way every piece of the kit, from the whole drum to the head to the hardware, would make a sound, could be translated into music. She played like she was having a conversation with the kit, and her band, and the audience. She played like the music was inside her and in front of her and all around her, like it was spilling out of her.

I had never played like that. I was good. I knew, logically, technically, that I was. That when I'd backed Eric, I'd elevated him, like he'd elevated me, and we'd created music that made people feel something. I knew I'd never played like Ava did, though. Not because she was technically better at it than me, although I thought she was. But because she loved it with her whole being. I loved it, but I kept part of myself back from it. It wasn't something I *needed*.

What I had needed, I thought, was to be with Eric. To be his best friend. To tie my life to his. I didn't know what to tie my life to now. It wasn't ever going to be Eric again, though. Eric was gone. He was never coming back. And he had left a hole in my life that I had been trying to fill and ignore at the same time. The thing was, I couldn't ignore it forever, any more than I could plaster over it with music or drumming, or not drumming. No matter what I did, no matter whether I ever played in another band or not, Eric would still be gone, missing from my life. Nothing was ever going to change that. That hurt. It hurt so much it made me want to double over with the force of it. But just . . . letting myself feel the edges of that hurt made it bearable too. Eric had died. But I had to keep going. And that was okay.

Drumming was a part of that, all tangled up in it. I missed drumming, and I missed being in a band, and I missed all the magical, impossible, life-affirming things that happened when you were in the very middle of that environment. When people responded to the things you created. I'd always miss it, like I was missing part of myself. But that was all right. I could miss it. It didn't mean that I needed to want it all back too.

Figuring that out, sitting behind the kit with the sticks resting on my knees, felt like the best thing that had happened to me in the last year. I felt guilty too, but more than anything, I felt free.

I played anyway, just because I wanted to. Because it felt good. Because, without everything else behind it, like there always had been before, it was only me and the drums and the music, and it made me happy. Because my mind would always be a drummer's mind, I'd always hear life in beats and rhythms, and I liked that. I played until my fingers ached and my hair dripped with sweat. I played loud and long, repeating anything that wasn't quite perfect, over and over, until I could feel the beats coursing through my veins like they were part of my blood. It was like, for one of the first times, I could actually hear myself. I could hear where I was good and where I needed work, but I didn't need to measure those things against myself, against my future. They were just pieces of the music I made.

I felt so good when I was done, my muscles all liquid-like with overuse, my skin washed clean with salty sweat, my hands still shaky from the impact of the sticks. So good, and so . . . flooded with new thoughts, and confused, and happy, and scared, all at the same time. I wanted to talk to someone. Just share this, a little bit. I wanted to call Eric, I realized. It was always him I'd gone to when I needed to work something out, tell someone something important. I thought about it while I showered, and when I came out of the bathroom, towel wrapped around my waist, I looked around, almost expecting to see him. I felt so stupid when I remembered that he was the last person I could tell about this. Even if he'd been here, alive, I didn't know if he'd want to hear this. That what he'd always wanted, so badly, wasn't what I wanted anymore. If he were alive, I wouldn't have been having this small epiphany at all. And that would have been okay too.

I felt myself shrink with the weight of what I'd half figured out, and the tumbling feeling of missing Eric, spreading over me, new, again. It happened all the time, that fresh realization that nothing would ever be the same, but I didn't think I'd ever get used to it, ever be able to brush it off.

I still needed to talk to someone, maybe even more now. I had friends I could call, people I could go hang out with. But I didn't know if they'd understand. No one had been close to Eric like I had. No one had really understood how important it had been for us to make music.

But Quinn had.

He picked up after two rings. "Micah? You okay?"

I realized then how odd it was for me to be calling him. I couldn't remember ever calling him before, except for when he'd been getting me the job with Escaping Indigo.

"I'm fine. I . . . I was drumming and . . ." I didn't know what to say. It all evaporated from my head.

There was a long pause on the other end of the line. Then he said, "Yeah." His voice was soft, raspy. "Are you okay?" he asked again, more gently than before, and I knew he understood. That I didn't have to say any more than that, if I didn't want to, because he already got it.

"Yeah." I slumped down into one of my kitchen chairs. The plastic was cool against my skin. "I feel . . . I feel pretty okay. I don't know. I looked for him. You know? I thought I'd turn around and he'd be there. I felt okay," I said again. "I wanted to tell him."

He sighed, his breath gusting through the phone line. "I'm glad you weren't feeling shitty, though. That's really good, kid."

"Yeah." And it was. I felt decent and that was a good thing. I realized I'd wanted someone to just . . . confirm that. To tell me it was all right. That I wasn't wrong, that it wasn't terrible of me to feel that way. That maybe things would be okay. "Thanks."

"Sure. Anytime." There was a scuffling noise on the other end of the phone, like he was sorting through something.

"Where are you?"

"Bellamy's."

"Oh." For a second there, for a few minutes while I was playing and having my tiny epiphany, I'd forgotten. I hadn't been angry and hurt. I hadn't missed Bellamy and wanted to push him away at the same time. My tangled feelings had been simple, and something I could figure out. But hearing Quinn say his name brought it all back. Something seemed to be constricting my heart, squeezing it tight. I closed my eyes and took a couple of deep breaths.

Another pause this time, weighty in a different way than the last. "Do you want to come over?"

I shook my head, even though he couldn't see me. "I don't think that's a good idea." But part of me wanted to say yes. Part of me wanted to go over and see Bellamy and . . . what? Yell at him some more so I'd feel better about the way he'd hurt me? Apologize so I'd feel better about the way I'd hurt him? I wasn't even sure. If I saw him, I wouldn't know what to say, where we stood with each other, and I didn't want to risk getting hurt all over again.

"Something happen between you two?" he asked, and I knew he was trying to be casual, but it didn't work at all.

"You're not as sneaky as you think."

He laughed, and it struck me that I couldn't remember hearing him ever do that before. Not for me, at least. Quinn and I didn't laugh together.

"I had an argument with him," I said. I didn't know if I was admitting it because of the laugh, or if I was admitting it because I wanted a friend.

He went quiet and thoughtful. "Do you want to tell me about it?"

I sighed. I hadn't realized I wanted him to ask that. I probably would have denied it, before. But it was like he'd taken a weight from me just by offering. "No. But thank you. Seriously."

"Okay. But if you want to . . ." He trailed off.

"Thanks."

"Look, I've got to go," he started. I was already nodding. My mind was still turning over everything I'd thought that day, though, everything I'd realized, everything I'd felt since I'd gotten home. And Bellamy. Bellamy was there, taking up all of my thoughts. Making the hurt come back with simply the mention of him. And I knew I couldn't do it. Suddenly, the idea of being on the road with him, which I'd been pushing to the back of my mind, seemed large and daunting and something I didn't want to face.

"Quinn," I said, quick, to stop him from hanging up, "can you handle those last festival dates by yourself?"

He was quiet for a long minute. "Did something come up? Or are you quitting?"

I pulled in air, wondered if I was thinking rationally, and then decided I didn't really care. I just didn't want to hurt anymore. "I think I'm quitting. I'm sorry. It's only a few more dates. And then you'll have time before they tour again, to find another roadie."

Quinn breathed heavily into the phone. "Well this is some seriously fucked-up déjà-vu."

I remembered then that this was pretty much exactly what had happened to Escaping Indigo's last roadie. That this was what Bellamy had been afraid of. But Bellamy and I had done this, messed this up, together.

"I'm sorry." I tried to squeeze some other words out, but nothing came. It was like there was a stone in my throat.

"Can you think about this for a few days, and then let me know what you really want?"

I opened my mouth to argue, but he kept talking before I could.

"If you really want it, it's fine." His words were gentle. "But I want to make sure. I want *you* to make sure."

"Okay," I agreed, but I was already letting the idea cement in my mind. I was already feeling lighter with it. And heavier and sadder, but Quinn didn't need to know that. The more I thought about this, the more sense it made. Everything would be easier this way. Bellamy could move on. I could move on.

"I'll talk to you later, okay?" He made it sound like a promise. We said good-bye and hung up. I wandered around my apartment for a while after that. I was lost, caught up in the past and the present and what I wanted for the future. Eventually I grabbed my sketchpad and drew all the empty spaces, where I could imagine Eric sitting or standing, turning toward me, or turning away.

Quinn showed up at my place the next day. I hadn't been expecting him—I wasn't expecting anyone, but Quinn never came around unless his mother needed something. But after the conversation we'd had the day before, I wasn't as surprised to see him. Still surprised, but I was starting to think that Quinn liked being the one who took care of everyone when they needed someone to lean on. It was what made him such a good person for Escaping Indigo to have around.

I'd left my door open. I'd been drumming, and the single-room apartment had gotten stuffy. In this heat, just opening the windows wasn't really enough. I was lying on my bed, headphones in, the door directly across from me, a bit of a cross breeze blowing over me, when he came up the stairs.

I pulled the earbuds out.

He hovered by the door. "You'll get mugged if you leave the door open, you know. This neighborhood."

I shrugged. "Not much for anyone to take."

His eyes flicked to the drum set.

"Like to see someone try," I told him.

A small smile played across his face. He gestured to the phone in my hands. "What are you listening to?"

I pulled the headphone plug out and let Bellamy's voice, Tuck's guitars, Ava's thumping drums spill out of the tinny phone speakers. Quinn grimaced, and I hit the Pause button, putting a stop to that sweet, harsh sound, those poetic lyrics, all those minor chords.

"Even though you just spent weeks listening to them?" he asked.

"Yeah." I twisted and set the phone and the headphones on the bedside table. I didn't put any force behind the word. "They don't stop being my favorite band because I know them now." It wasn't a lie, but truthfully, it was odd to listen to their music now. I'd been about to change the song before Quinn came in. Hearing Bellamy singing was too real and raw. And listening to Escaping Indigo was a bit different too. Not in a bad way. But as if I was seeing it from a different perspective. Like I was standing next to it instead of apart from it. I couldn't help analyzing Bellamy's lyrics in a totally new way, either. Couldn't help seeing him in every word he sang.

Quinn sighed and took another step into the room. "I know that, Micah. I really do." He gestured at the table and chairs in the corner opposite the drums. "Can I . . . ?"

I nodded. "Yeah, sorry, of course."

He grabbed a chair and swung it around so he could straddle it, his arms across the top. I swiveled to face him.

He rubbed at the back of his neck, like he wasn't quite sure how to start. "I really think you should go and see him," he blurted out. "And maybe you can . . . talk about this, so I don't have to get a new roadie."

I shook my head. "I really don't think it's a good idea." I didn't. The words stuck a little, though. I'd had a day to think about it, and I didn't want to take it back. But it did make me sad, sadder than I'd have imagined, to think about not going back on the road with Escaping Indigo. With Quinn and Ava and Tuck and Lissa. With Bellamy. Bellamy, who I might have been starting to fall for. I'd found a place there, of sorts. With the band. With him. The first place that had felt like it was just mine, not something that was all tied up with Eric. And now I had to give it away because it hurt too much. Part of me didn't want to do it at all, wanted to tell Quinn I had changed my mind. It wasn't a small part, either.

But it did hurt, and this would make it easier. It would be best this way.

"He's been . . . miserable since we got home, Micah. I didn't know why. He's usually pretty down after a tour ends, but this was worse." He cocked his head a bit, eyeing me. "Now I think I get it. You should talk."

I slumped back against the wall. "I don't know. We can't . . . We can't seem to do that. Talk."

"About what?"

"About anything. Quinn . . ." I narrowed my eyes at him, a thought occurring to me. "Why do you care what happens between the two of us? If we work out? You can find another roadie. We're not exactly a rare breed."

He straightened in his seat. "I don't care, if you both don't want it to work out."

"Actually," I went on, ignoring what he'd said while I remembered the conversation we'd had that day outside the venue, about Bellamy. "Actually, you warned me off him."

"I didn't warn you off him," he said, sharp and slightly irritated.

I raised my eyebrows, and he looked down. "Close enough," I said.

"I just wanted you to be careful. I didn't want you hurt."

I bit back what I'd been about to say. He sounded defensive, but he also sounded like he was telling the truth. "Why? Why do you care?"

Quinn shrugged. His gaze was on the floor. "Were you in love with Eric?"

My heart thumped hard in my chest. "No." It was the truth, but it hurt to say, and I wasn't sure why.

Quinn glanced back up at me. I think, if I'd passed him on the street right then, I wouldn't have recognized him. His face was so open, his eyes so wide, and for the first time, I thought I could really see the hole Eric had left in him. The deep grief and, maybe even more, the confusion. "Was he in love with you?" he asked.

I shook my head. As far as I'd known, Eric had been straight. But either way, I knew he had never felt that way about me. It had never been like that between us. I said as much out loud.

Quinn took a deep breath, pushed his hands through his hair. It flopped back down over his face, shielding his eyes, the dark strands stark against his pale skin. For a second, I saw the beauty in him. I'd always looked at him in the way I supposed someone would look at a family member—I couldn't see him objectively. He was just Quinn, just Eric's brother. But there was a fineness to his strength, a beauty in the shape of his lips and his eyes and the way he was so determined to look at me, even though it was clear he was uncomfortable.

"You're part of my life." His voice was a low rumble. I had to lean forward to hear him. "You always were. But . . ." He shrugged, an uneven roll of his shoulders. "Eric's not here. And I am. And there's . . ." He smiled, a quick flash. "There's a lot between us."

I shook my head. "And that . . . what? Makes it important for you to watch out for me?"

He bit his lip. It was an odd expression on his face. He had such a tough-guy look going on. It was strange to see him vulnerable, unsure. This whole conversation was strange.

"No," he said. "*You* make it important. I care about what happens to you."

My mouth opened and closed. "Oh."

He swallowed uncomfortably. "Yeah."

What was I supposed to say here? "Thanks." I found I meant it. What he was saying was surprising, definitely, but not unwanted. And I realized that, if I dug deep enough into myself, beyond hurt and beyond the past itself, I felt the same. He was part of my life. We hadn't picked it, but that didn't make it untrue. "Thank you."

He nodded, and there were a few moments of strained, awkward silence, neither of us knowing what to say.

Finally, he cleared his throat. "So, *do* you want it?"

"What?" I asked, looking back up at him. "A relationship with Bellamy?"

He nodded.

I sighed, and he raised his eyebrows at me. "I don't think he wants to be with me," I said.

He smiled, slow and wide, and sly, like he knew things I didn't. "That's not what I asked. And I think you're wrong."

I narrowed my eyes at him. "How would you know?"

He took a breath, letting the smile and the knowing look go. "I told you he's having a thing. Like what he had on tour? Except . . . not as visible. But maybe worse, because he's keeping it all inside."

"What kind of thing?"

Quinn shrugged. "I'm not an expert. But sometimes, especially when he's overemotional or when . . . when we come home and there's no tour for him to look forward to, or when he's trying to write new stuff for an album, he gets . . . He goes into his own head and won't come out. He functions. So it's hard to see. But it's there. Just because he hides it doesn't mean it isn't there."

I pressed my lips together, thinking, all my thoughts swirling so hard and so fast I couldn't grab hold and make them make sense. "He told me . . . something about that."

Quinn nodded, like he was encouraging me, or urging me toward something. "That's how I know. He doesn't tell anyone. If he told you . . ." He trailed off and let the sentence hang, but his eyes were wide, as if he wanted me to understand something.

"That's what started this whole fight with him, though," I argued.

He leaned forward, tipping up the back legs of his chair. I was afraid he was going to break the thing in his eagerness to tell me whatever it was he needed to get out. "Look . . . sometimes, he hurts people because *he's* hurting."

I frowned. "That's not a ringing endorsement."

"I'm not done." He brushed his hand through the air, chopping my words out of the way. "I think he's afraid of that. He did it to his last boyfriend—they were *always* at each other's throats. They never saw eye to eye and that boy wanted to fix Bellamy, and he couldn't. It doesn't work that way, it's never going to. That guy was an idiot, but he meant well for a lot of it." He sighed.

I twisted my fingers together. My legs were dangling off the edge of the bed, and I wanted to kick them like a little kid. "I get not wanting to be hurt." I did. There were a lot of things, I was beginning to see, that I couldn't truly understand about Bellamy. I could try, but I couldn't really get there. But I understood pain. I understood wanting to avoid that feeling of loss at any cost. I understood thinking that if it happened again, if I ever had to feel like that again, if I had pain piled on top of pain, I might not make it through.

I got that.

I looked up at Quinn, and I knew he got it too. He was staring at me, just watching me, like he was waiting for me to come to all those conclusions on my own. He knew how I felt. He was, except for his mother, maybe the only person on the planet who could understand how I felt. How it was to lose a brother. How it was to pick your life back up again when it seemed like a huge part of you was missing.

"Bellamy said I couldn't let go of Eric." I kept looking down at my hands. I couldn't look at Quinn while I said this. I was . . . ashamed, but I wasn't sure exactly why. Because part of me wanted to be able to let go, part of me wanted to leave Eric behind so he couldn't hurt me anymore, and that felt so infinitely wrong. "I said . . . I said he thought I was going to be just like his ex, and he said I thought he was going to be just like Eric. He said the only reason I wasn't drumming in a new band was because of Eric. He said I couldn't let go."

Quinn was quiet for so long that I glanced up, only to find him staring a hole into the floor.

"Quinn?"

He shook his head, like he was coming back to himself. "We're never going to be able to let go. You know that, right? You know it's always going to hurt?"

I hesitated, but Quinn didn't wait for me to agree or disagree.

"I think Bellamy will listen if you talk to him," he said, gently. "I think . . . he's scared, like I said. I think he likes you a lot, Micah." He smiled lopsidedly at me. "I think he's afraid to hope you'll be different, because then he might get attached. I know he's difficult. I know he hurt you. But I don't think he meant it. I've known him for a long time." He tilted his head to the side, as if he was coming to his own new conclusions about Bellamy. "I know that he's worth it. Every time he's . . . He's worth it."

I smiled back. It felt wobbly and fragile on my face, like I'd have to work to keep it there. "I know he is." I closed my eyes and tipped my head back.

"What do you want, Micah?" Quinn asked, his voice soft. He sounded honestly curious. "I know it hurts. I know it's scary. But . . . what do *you* need? What do you want? Eric isn't here. It's all you from here on out."

I hesitated. It took me a long moment, because just thinking about it was terrifying. And it felt wrong, in a way, too. Like if I was saying what I wanted, then I was as good as admitting that Eric wasn't there anymore to make choices with me.

But it had been a long time since anyone had asked me that. I'd let people direct me for so long, and it had been good. It had never been anything I *didn't* want. But I couldn't remember the last time I'd decided I'd wanted something, just for me.

"I don't know," I admitted. "Not . . . not this. But I don't know what."

Quinn stood up and pushed his chair in. "Maybe . . . talk to him, then?" He ran his hand through his hair. "If you still want to leave the band after, that's okay. Just don't . . . let this slip away without at least talking to him."

I nodded. I could do that. I could at least try. "Okay."

chapter thirteen

X

It probably was simple, for most people, to pick up a phone and call someone. But I almost felt like I'd forgotten how. I kept walking around with the phone in my hand, running through potential conversations in my mind. I didn't know what to say. Whether I wanted to yell at him or apologize or tell him all over again that I didn't need or want him to be perfect, any more than he needed me to be perfect. I wasn't actually sure, still, that I wanted to talk to him at all. But every time I put the phone down, I picked it back up again. What Quinn had said, about letting Bellamy slip away without a fight, kept echoing in my mind. I'd let Eric slip away like that. I didn't want to do that again, even if it was painful. Even if nothing came from it.

I was walking back and forth, between my kitchen and my bed, weaving around the bass drum sticking out into the open living room with each pass, when I finally got up the nerve and hit Dial. It rang three times, and I think I died about a million times in the space of those seconds before he answered.

"Micah?"

"Hey." Ridiculous, that I couldn't think of anything better. After all that thinking and planning of words, and that was what I came out with. *Hey.* But it seemed like maybe it was the right thing to say, because he sighed into the phone in a breathy way.

I took a deep breath. "I need . . . I want to talk to you. Can we talk?"

He didn't say anything for a second, but it was only a second. "I talked to Quinn. He said you want to quit."

"I'm thinking about it," I said softly. "But I'd like to talk to you first."

This time he was quiet for longer. "Okay. I want that too."

I breathed out, far more relieved than I'd thought I would be. My lungs loosened up enough for me to speak. "Can I see you, actually? Can we do this face-to-face instead of over the phone?" I hadn't planned to ask that, but now that we were talking, now that I could hear his voice, it seemed so important that I be able to see his face too. Look him in the eye so I could be sure that I said what I wanted, that I saw his expressions. Whether this all went right or wrong.

"Yeah," he said, the word slipping out on a sigh. "Do you want to come here? There's . . . there's a park by my house. We can meet there if you want, and then you won't be stuck in my house if . . ." He trailed off. That made some sense to me, so I agreed. Bellamy gave me the address, and I headed over.

Bellamy's neighborhood was a quiet one. Not really someplace you'd expect someone in a relatively successful band to live, I supposed, but unless they were at the very pinnacle of success, bands never made as much as anyone assumed. And San Diego was an expensive place, even, I thought, in a suburb like this. Ava had a place much closer to the beach, and I bet she'd dropped a lot of cash on it. Bellamy's house, here, wouldn't have been quite as much, but these places were big and new and pretty. It was nice, invisible in the grand scheme of things. Perfect for someone who wanted to live somewhere they wouldn't be noticed.

Bellamy met me at the edge of the park, right by the road where I'd parked, and we walked in together. It wasn't as awkward as I'd thought it would be. We didn't touch, or even say much, but it reminded me of walking through that park at the festival with him, of the way he'd led me through the trees, to our own place where we could be alone, and together.

I wanted it to be like this, I realized. I wanted easiness between us. I didn't need us to be happy all the time. I didn't mind if Bellamy was sad, or worried, or scared, or nervous, or anxious, if he was so down that he couldn't see his way back up. I didn't *want* him to feel that, any of that. I wanted things to be good for him. But he didn't have to be happy for me to love him. This, this easiness, this was good.

He led me through a big grass field and past a line of tall trees, so most of the park was hidden from the road. There was a playground off to one side, with one of those metal slides that looked both amazing and completely lethal at the same time, and a swing set. Bellamy headed right for the swings. He sat on one and started kicking his legs back and forth. I sat on the one next to him.

I hadn't been on a swing in a long time. Years, maybe. But it was like riding a bike. I sat down and my body knew what to do. And my heart remembered, all over again, why I loved swinging. The rush of it. The intense feeling of soaring and falling and the slight, tingly fear that I could fall right out of the air but never did. I didn't think we were swinging very high, but when I got to the top of the arc, it was like I was sitting in the sky, on top of the world, like I could reach out and touch every single thing I could see. Like I was a giant and my heart was as big as the space around me. The rush of excitement pounded in my veins, pulsed through my blood. It made me want to laugh out loud.

When I came back down, I passed Bellamy as he was going up, and all the way back, I could watch him, flying into that same sky. The strong lines of his back, of his knees and calves, his feet dangling in their sneakers—he was a dark silhouette against the clouds. His hands gripped the chains of the swing, his whole body flexed as he pushed off. His spine was straight, his head up, and I wondered if he was feeling anything like the pure, unstoppable delight that I was.

After a while we slowed, until the arcs we were making were small, and we were beside each other more and more. The sun was setting across from us, and when I looked over at Bellamy, the sunset turned his hair gold and red and splashed light on his skin, like he'd been painted in watercolors.

I was a bit giddy. It had to be some kind of craziness, to want to fling yourself up into the sky and back down toward the ground, but it made me feel wonderful. It made me feel like I was alive.

He turned his face so that he was watching the sunset and not me. His feet dragged against the ground when he came to the middle of his arc, and he jerked them up. "I'm sorry."

I coughed. "*You're* sorry?"

He did turn to me then, a wrinkle forming between his brows as he frowned. "Yeah. What?"

"*I'm* sorry." I held up my hand before he could interrupt. "No, I am. I said some really awful things, and I didn't mean them. I was..." I laughed, remembering what Quinn had said about Bellamy being afraid, what Bellamy himself had said. "I was scared." Fear made us say and do things that would have seemed impossible. It was what had been driving us the entire time we'd known each other. I wanted it to stop. "I didn't understand—I don't understand why you don't want to get help, if you can. I don't... I can't be the first person to suggest it."

He sighed through his nose and kicked his feet against the scuffed-up dirt below the swing. "You're not. And I do understand the point you're making. It's just... It's my choice. I still get a choice. I don't even like talking about it. I don't... I don't like people looking at me and seeing... someone who's damaged."

"You're not damaged," I said quickly, because I knew he wasn't, no matter how his mind worked. But my own mind was turning the words over and over. I pressed my hands together, tightened my fingers around themselves. It didn't seem right. But when Bellamy had told me that I was the one who needed to see someone, that I needed help because I wasn't dealing with my grief, it had stung. It had felt as if he'd attacked me. Even though he might have been right. Even though he probably *had been* right. I'd been embarrassed, and I'd felt like he was saying there was something wrong with me. I hadn't meant to make him feel that way. I had only wanted to help.

I didn't like it. I wouldn't ever, probably. I didn't want Bellamy to hurt, and there were things he could try, but maybe he never would. But when I tried to put aside what I was feeling, and see it from Bellamy's point of view, I could almost understand. It was his choice. It would always be his choice. And whether he got help, or we all stood by him, or whatever else happened, he'd be the one to make the choices to manage, or not manage, this. I'd told Bellamy that I needed to make *my* own choices about life. It shouldn't be any different for him. I'd promised Bellamy that he could trust me. If that meant him taking his own way to handle this thing, then I'd be okay with that. Because I knew I needed to handle Eric's loss in *my* own way. I'd realized that yesterday. Or maybe I'd been starting to realize it for a while. Maybe it had been settling in my mind all this time and had only, finally, hit home yesterday. They were different things, but I could see the parallels.

He shook his head. "I know I'm not damaged. You were right, though." He twisted his chin a little, as if thinking, then turned back to me. "I let this thing rule me. I let the fear of what it can do rule me."

"I'm so sorry for saying that. I don't think that, really. I think it's just a thing that happens in your mind."

"I know." He sounded like he did. Like it had been said and I'd apologized and now it was over. "The same as I'm sorry for saying you were using me to replace Eric. I know you're not, Micah. I do."

I took a deep breath, to speak, but then I didn't know what to say. I was still angry about that. Or maybe not angry, but hurt. Tender in a place that was already wounded. Maybe more so because in some ways, Bellamy was right. Sometimes I wanted Eric back so much I couldn't see anything. Not what I wanted. Not what I needed. Not even Bellamy.

"Eric would know what to do," I said. Bellamy blinked. "You would have liked him. And . . . he'd have known what to do. He'd have been at my back."

Bellamy was quiet for a bit. Then he said, "I'm sorry you have to live without him, Micah. But other people will have your back now. I promise."

I nodded. Quinn had said almost the same thing, or implied it, and it was true. And I was so grateful for it. But no one was ever going to replace Eric for me. No feeling was ever going to replace what I felt for him. I knew that, clearly, now. That was okay. But it still hurt.

Bellamy's hands slid down the chains of the swing. "I don't really think you need to let go of Eric," he said softly. "I shouldn't have said that."

I tipped my head back so I could see the sky. "You were right about a lot of it." I'd thought about it all, so much, over the last couple of days. The thing was, I'd never really done that before. I'd never given myself a moment to figure out what missing Eric, what losing him, meant in a long-term way. All I'd ever considered was how badly it hurt, and how much I didn't know what to do without him. Quinn had been right, though—Eric wasn't coming back, and I had to accept that. And then I had to figure out how to live without him. I had to rely on other people. Quinn. The band, maybe. Bellamy. "As much as your anxiety takes its toll on you, missing Eric takes a toll on me," I said, slow, trying to work through what I was feeling and put it into the right words.

Bellamy nodded. "I know. That's why I shouldn't have said that. I don't expect you to forget him, Micah. I'd never ask that. I was just…"

"You don't want to be him. You don't want me to think you're going to hurt me in the same way he did." I turned to the side and gave him a tiny smile. He blushed.

"And you don't want me to think you're going to be like my ex."

"Do you?" I asked. "Do you think I'll do that?"

He shrugged. "I don't know. I like you, Micah. But we don't actually know each other that well. I know you enough to know that if you *did* act like him, though, it would hurt so much. I just can't deal with that, not when I'm still… dealing with him leaving and the end of the tour and having to write a new album. It's too much stress. And the band comes first."

I nodded. I got that. Bellamy wasn't the only one depending on Escaping Indigo. It was his livelihood, but also Ava's, and Tuck's, and Quinn's, and Lissa's, to an extent. There was a lot riding on it.

"You weren't wrong, though," I said. "I need to deal with it. And I wasn't dealing with it well."

He kicked his sneakers along the dirt under the swing and kept his gaze there. "I'm not either. And you weren't wrong. I need… I need to do something about this." He swallowed hard and looked down at his knees. "I called Ava. I was so… fucking confused. I didn't know what to do. How to make you come back. How to make this work."

My heart beat harder at *make this work*. If he wanted that, I'd do anything. I'd stand beside him no matter what, I'd do my best, try my hardest. I just wanted it so bad.

"What did Ava say?" I asked, trying to focus on that and not jump down his throat to ask him if he really wanted this and if we could be together. Trying not to let any of it overwhelm me.

He smiled, a tiny, sweet thing. "She said I could compromise. She also said I was nuts and I should probably do something about it, because why not?"

I swallowed. "And that's okay with you?"

He nodded. "I don't think I'm nuts. I think this is . . . just me. But I do think that it's not . . . That things aren't as good as they could be. I want to be with you. I want . . . I want to try. I'd do pretty much anything to make that happen."

I breathed and tried to just be relieved. "I don't think you're nuts either. I don't. But I think . . . there might be something out there that could help. And if you don't like it, you don't have to keep doing whatever it is."

"I don't want to take anything. I just *don't*." He spit the word out, and I leaned back a little. Then I remembered that this was all new, and it was a big step, him even thinking about doing something. I reached out and took his hand, pulling it away from the swing's chain. I tugged him toward me a little, so our swings bumped, then swung apart.

"Okay. You don't have to. That can't be the only option." I'd heard good things about medications for this type of thing, but the truth was, I didn't know anything much about any of this, either. It was all stuff said in passing. What Quinn, what Bellamy himself, had said was still forefront in my mind—that it was Bellamy's choice. That it would all have to be Bellamy's choice. And there had to be other ways to do something about this, other ways for him to get help. "Wouldn't it be good to have someone to talk to, though? Maybe?"

He bit at his lip. "I have you. And the band. And Quinn and Lissa."

"We're not impartial, though. I'm not impartial, sweetheart. And . . . you don't talk to us. Not as often as any of us want. Not as often as you probably need, and not about the stuff you really need to say. But maybe if you could talk to someone who was impartial, who was just there to listen, to be a mirror, then you *could* talk to me, and the band, and your friends. Maybe you could get this stuff off your chest instead of holding it all in. Maybe it would . . . make it easier to get through it when you're anxious or down or whatever." I didn't want to push him into this. I just wanted him to be happy.

"What will they tell me?" He sounded half-exasperated and half-terrified. "That I have to just get through it? Think positive? I already know that. I don't need bullshit platitudes."

I squeezed his hand. "I know you don't. But you don't know what they'll say. And if it doesn't work, you don't have to go back. You can try something else. Or nothing at all. Bellamy, I want you to be happy, and I want you to . . . not be afraid to be with someone. Me," I said, because, at this point, we both knew what I meant. "But anyone. And this could help. But if you really don't want to do this, if you want to deal with this on your own like you have been, it's okay." I took a deep breath, and he looked at me, looked me in the eye while I spoke. It made everything easier and more difficult at the same time. "It's your choice. Not mine. Not anyone else's. Not right now. I don't want you to do it because you think I want you to, or Ava wants you to, or anyone. I want you to do it for yourself. If you're not ready for that, that's okay. If you're never ready for that, it's okay."

He let go of my hand, fast enough that when our swings sprang apart, they swung back so our hips bumped again. "No," he said, and for a second, my heart stuttered in my chest. "I think . . . I think if we're going to do this. You and me." He turned to me and moved his hand in a circle between us. I smiled, because otherwise, I thought I was going to cry. "If we're going to, I could think about trying that. Maybe. I think I might need to. And . . . I might want to. For me."

"That works for me," I told him. He smiled at me.

"I wouldn't mind having some control over the anxiety," Bellamy said, and his smile went a bit wry, his mouth lifting at one side. "I really wouldn't."

"I know."

"It's a bad thing," he said after a long minute. His voice was soft but sure. The way he said it, I could almost hear the capitalization of the word *bad*. Such a simple word. But I knew it was the worst thing he could think of to describe it—it was simple and awful. "It tells me that, just because I did something once—wrote a song, wrote an album, had success—it doesn't mean I can do it again. It tells me that maybe this will fail. That maybe everything will fall apart. Not only the band, or the music, but everything. You. Us. Everything."

He glanced at me, and one side of his smile quirked up. "I know how weird that sounds. How illogical. I know it doesn't run on a schedule or look like what anyone expects it to look like, and that makes it hard to believe. But that's just . . . It's how it works." He reached up, ran a hand through his hair. "I can feel it in me, weighing on me, but there's nothing I can do about it. Knowing it's there, knowing it'll go away eventually, doesn't mean I can make it less real right now. I know I just have to get through it, but getting through it is *hard*."

I did understand that. I was starting to, at least. And he was right. I'd expected it to look and act a certain way, and it never had. I'd expected it to be predictable. I'd expected big things to set it off. I'd expected it to be controllable, and it wasn't. Not right now.

He took a deep breath, and it shuddered through him, shaking him. "I don't want to do it anymore. I want it to go away."

I nodded. I didn't know what to say. I didn't want to say anything foolish and ruin this, because it was so important. "I might see someone too." My voice was soft, because it made me nervous, and maybe I understood, just a little bit, what Bellamy was saying. "A grief counselor or something. Just . . . someone to talk to."

He nodded. "That might be good." He glanced up, and held my eyes. "Why aren't you in a new band, really? Is it truly all because of Eric?"

I thought about playing yesterday, how good it had felt. How different. How I'd known that it wasn't the center that held me together anymore. "Some of it's because of Eric," I told him. "Most of it's just me, though. I . . . My life changed. And now that piece doesn't fit anymore." I pushed off a little, swung a bit out, a bit back. "I don't think it was ever really about being in a band or not, Bellamy. I think it was about figuring out how to live without him. Figuring out . . . that I have to live without him. Trying to put something in the place he had been. Fill that hole."

"And have you figured it out?" he asked, so soft I almost couldn't hear him.

"That I have to live without him?" God, it was hard to say. I didn't think it would ever get easier. I didn't think I *wanted* it to get easier. "Yes. How I do that? Not . . . not so much." I gave him a wobbly smile, and he returned it. "But I can work on that."

"We could work on things together?" His voice was so sincere I almost wanted to laugh, but it was so honest it cut into me too. "Unless . . . do you really want to leave the band? Do you want to end this?"

I shook my head. "No, Bellamy. I want to stay." I'd always wanted that. I just hadn't wanted it if I wasn't wanted back.

He reached out and took my hand, fingers wrapping tight around mine, and his smile went soft and sweet. He went back to swinging, not as high as before, and sometimes we kicked off to the side, so our swings bumped and we could touch.

He glanced at me. "You don't think less of me. Because I have this thing. Whatever it is."

I shook my head. "No. It makes me nervous. I don't want you . . ." I took a deep breath. "It hurts to see you when you're low, Bellamy. It hurts that your ex used this against you and left you . . . scared." Scared to trust, scared to be with anyone—that was the part I got the most. Eric hadn't meant to desert me, but he had. And when he'd gone, it had broken the thing inside me that let me lean on a relationship— whether that relationship was with a friend, a brother, a lover. "I don't think less of you. I just don't want you in pain."

He gazed back out at the sky. The sun was dipping down, getting lower, lengthening shadows as the afternoon stretched out. It was quiet out here. A car passed every now and then, but for the most part, it felt like we were completely alone. Like we'd been, that night, when we'd smoked behind the venue. Or when I'd held Bellamy for the first time, in the dark of the tour bus. We were always making spaces for us.

"I didn't want anyone to try to fix me," he said, so soft I had to lean toward him to hear. "I hate everything about being . . . like this. Anxious. Depressed. Fucked up. Whatever you want to call it." He was staring straight ahead again, but his hands were in his lap this time, not wrapped so tightly around the chains. "I hate feeling it, and I hate what it does to me and how I can't explain it, and when I try, people look at me like talking about it is what makes me nuts. I just, when I'm in it, I just want it to stop. I feel so empty. And it hurts so much."

He looked over at me. His eyebrows drew together over his nose. "But it . . . it gives me something to build on." His mouth flicked up in a quick smile again, a real one this time. Then it faded. "I know that's messed up. I know how bad that sounds. And I don't ever want to feel this way again. I never do. But when I look back, I can't exactly regret that it happened. I regret how I am and what I've said and even what I've done. But it's part of me, part of who I am. It . . . shaped me. And it reminds me that I'm alive. That this—" He waved his hand, taking in us and the swings and the park and the sunset in front of us, but maybe he meant even more than that. Maybe he meant everything. "That it's not permanent. That it's special. That it means something."

I thought about how hard it had once been, when I first started playing, to hear the drum parts in a song, separate from all the other music. If I'd wanted to know what the bass drum was doing, or the crash, or what the individual beats were in a fill, I'd had to listen so hard. I'd thought of it like diving into a black well. Closing my eyes and sinking into the music like it was water that covered me and filled my nose and my eyes and my lungs, until I reached the very bottom. And there the sounds I'd been searching for would be, tucked together, waiting for me to pull them out so I could play them right. It hadn't been that difficult in a long time. Now, if I wanted to know what a drummer was doing in a song, if I wanted to play along, those sounds were floating right on top, just there, mostly easy to grab so I could sort them out. I never forgot that image, though. The blackness in it. The beauty and the excitement and the sweet success after the struggle. I thought that even if I never felt that again— the sinking into the dark—the memory of it made everything else, all the easier things that came after, mean more. Maybe, in a small way, that was similar to what Bellamy was trying to describe.

Maybe it was similar to navigating the hole Eric had left in me. Not the same—I couldn't understand, truly, what Bellamy was feeling, and he couldn't understand what I was. But I knew, even with all the pain, even with all the times I wished it would stop, that I'd never regret knowing and loving Eric. I just had to start trying not to regret all the hurt that came with it.

Bellamy had started swinging again, a tiny rise and fall of movement. As if what he'd just said wasn't the most honest and horrible and amazing thing I'd ever heard. I stayed still. I wasn't sure I could take my eyes off him.

"The bitter and the sweet?" I asked.

He nodded. "Yeah."

I sighed, not because I was exasperated, or tired, or worn out, but because the idea that he was afraid to lose that broke my heart. "No one's going to try to take your emotions away, Bellamy. I promise. I won't let it happen."

He seemed surprised, and laughed, and I felt ridiculously good to have done it. And he smiled at me, a tiny bit sheepish, and I thought I might have said the right thing too, this once.

We swung for a while longer and didn't talk about anything anymore. No more about what went on in his head, no more about what we were doing together, no more apologizing. I wanted to apologize again. I was still sick over the things I'd said in anger. And even though he'd dismissed it, I thought he'd be going over those words in his mind, when he was anxious, when he was wondering if we were doing the right thing by wanting to try to be together. I didn't want him to have to wonder. I wanted him to know.

But, for now, I let it go. We stayed out until the sun started to set, just the two of us. I looked over at him. He was staring off into the distance, his legs kicking idly to make the swing rock back and forth.

"Bellamy?"

"Mmm?" He turned to me, and there he was. The rock star. The setting sun was turning his hair dark gold, shadowing his skin, highlighting him just like the lights on stage did. But it wouldn't have mattered, because he was beautiful and striking and arresting, completely captivating, without any of that. He was holding himself straight, his shoulders back, his chin up. He looked proud, and even though I was pretty sure that most of that was a defensiveness, a forced, casual certainty he wrapped himself in to keep himself safe, I couldn't help but think that he looked strong and sure. Just the fact that he *wanted* to be seen that way seemed strong to me. Brave.

He hadn't been focused on me until I said his name, and I watched him switch his attention, watched his gaze go from far away to me. And it felt like magic. Like I couldn't possibly be this lucky, that he would look at me like that, give me that attention. It didn't seem possible that he'd look at me with so much want. But he did. He was.

"Can we go home?" I asked, and he nodded and smiled at me, and I held out my hand.

chapter fourteen

It was different than before, this time. It wasn't rushed. We weren't frantic. There was a quiet desperation behind it, though, in the way we touched each other, the way neither of us wanted to let go long enough to get clothes off, get up the stairs to the bedroom. Maybe because we'd missed each other, the closeness we'd had, so much. Maybe because it was different, this time. Before, we'd told ourselves—I had, at least—that I couldn't let it mean as much as I wanted. That I couldn't be sure of what Bellamy wanted, so I couldn't let myself get lost in it as much as I might have. But now things had changed. Whatever was between was, if not solid, at least real, and something we could build on.

It wasn't planned, really. But when we got to Bellamy's house, I caught him right before the door, and kissed him. He just looked so lovely, so pale and fragile and beautiful. And he kissed back. And then we didn't stop, couldn't stop, but it didn't feel like the wrong thing to do. It felt like the only option, right then.

His fingers shook a little, a tremble running through his hands, when we finally got to the bedroom, and he slid his palms under my shirt, pulled the hem up and over my head to take it off me. I was surprised, and then I wasn't. I was nervous too.

I slipped my hands under his T-shirt, dipped my hands into the back of his jeans, while he fumbled with the button on mine. He couldn't get it undone, and he laughed, embarrassed, against my neck. I pulled him closer. I kissed him again, moved my hands around and undid his jeans instead. He moaned into my mouth when I touched him, but he didn't move away, didn't stop the kiss. His lips moved over mine in a slow way, his tongue tasting me. It wasn't like any kiss we'd had before. It was unhurried, a deep and deliberate exploration of the ways we could fit together.

It was a while before we broke apart. Eventually, he stepped back enough that I could get his shirt off, and we could do away with the rest of our clothes, leaving them in haphazard puddles on the floor. He turned us, pulling at my hips, tugging me along, and we landed on the bed, Bellamy under me. His hands slid over my back and my shoulders and my chest, down to my stomach, over my hip bones. His fingers never stopped moving, exploring my skin, finding all the hollows and soft spots, the places that made me breathless. I wanted to do the same, wanted to know every piece of him, know what he liked, where he wanted me.

I kissed down the line of his throat. He tipped his head back against the pillows, and I kissed to his collarbone, then the center of his chest. He had a smattering of freckles under one nipple, and I detoured to lick them, trying to taste their texture on my tongue. He squirmed under me. A laugh burst out of him, and I looked up. He seemed surprised that he'd made the noise, his face flushed, his eyes wide, but he met my smile with a small one of his own. His hands buried into my hair, tugging me back to the spot.

I went, kissing the freckles for a minute, but then I kept going, moving over his body, tasting whatever caught my attention. I mouthed the sharp swells of his hips, the edges of his rib cage, rising and falling in gasps, the inside of his wrist when he dropped it low enough for me to reach. My hands moved across his thighs, around to his hips to hold him still. I paused when I got low enough that the head of his cock nudged at my throat. I moved up and down over it, rubbing myself against the tender skin, letting him feel the roughness of my stubble. He moaned, loud, and when I glanced up, his head was thrown to the side, his eyes squeezed shut.

I slipped a bit lower and took him into my mouth, tasting the salty bitterness of him. He was thick and heavy on my tongue. I tried to swallow him, felt him in the back of my throat. I wanted all of him, wanted to hold him inside me. He bucked his hips up when I tightened my throat around him, twisted in the sheets when I drew away, then sank back down on him, when I pressed my lips to the crown.

"Micah." His voice was a rasp, no real sound to it.

I pulled off him, his cock slipping out of my mouth with a wet sound that made me shiver. "Okay?"

He twisted to the side, almost out of my reach. I held him in place, one hand flat on his hip, pressing down, the other under him, fingers digging in hard enough to bruise. I ducked my head so I could run my lips over his balls, take one into my mouth. His hips twitched hard, and he cried out, the sound going from high and shocked to low and desperate, drawn out while I sucked on him.

"Micah. Micah, please." His hands were bunched in the bedding, his fingers white.

I sat back, feet tucked under me, knees spread so it would be impossible for him not to see how turned on I was. "What do you want?"

He opened his eyes and peered up at me from under his sweat-soaked bangs. He slid his gaze over me. His hips bucked up again, and an answering jolt ran through my cock. He was gorgeous and impossible, all spread out in front of me, slicked with sweat and my kisses, red marks on his skin from where I'd moved my mouth over him, his body twisted with want, open to whatever I wanted to do with him.

We stared at each other, and a tightness grew in my chest the longer he looked at me like that, like he was taking root there. Like I'd never be able to get him out. Then he rolled onto his stomach and spread his legs. He propped himself up on his elbows and turned to gaze back at me. His shoulders twitched in a tiny shrug, like he was daring me, but his eyes looked uncertain.

I kissed the base of his spine, slipped my hands down over him, and he shuddered. He dropped his head between his arms. I couldn't stop touching him. I wanted to feel every single inch of his skin.

"Now, now, now," he said, his words more like gasps, over and over, like he couldn't stop.

"Where . . . Bellamy, stuff?" I was breathless with the want in him, with the answering desire in myself.

He reached around to the bedside table, pulled supplies out of the drawer, and tossed them back to me. I yanked open the condom and put it on, slicked myself. Then I leaned forward, covering him with my body, and pressed inside.

A tremor ran through him, shaking me as it shook him. I clamped a hand over his wrist, wrapped the other around his chest. He leaned back into me, canted his hips up to meet me, sliding me farther inside him. I barked out a groan, lowered my head to his shoulder, pressed my lips into his skin.

I wouldn't last, not after the time I'd spent working myself up while I'd done my best to drive him crazy. I moved inside him, and he pushed back, our bodies rocking. I sprawled over him, never drawing very far away, and he arched up into me, against me, our skin sliding together. The way we were pressed together didn't allow for a lot of movement, but I didn't care, and he didn't seem to either. It was more important, right then, to be close. I reached one hand under him and wrapped my fingers around his cock, smoothing them up and down, matching our rhythm. For a while, that's all there was—the movement of us, the ripples of our bodies against each other, me around him and him around me.

When he finally came, he seemed to do it in stages, like the sensations were coming from deep inside of him and spilling out slow and hard. His body tensed and flexed, and I felt him come over my hand, into the sheets. He moved against me, taking me farther into his body, clenching down around me, and I came after a few more thrusts. It was intense, like a static surge running through me, from my neck to the base of my spine, pulling everything out of me. I buried my face in his shoulder and yelled with the feel of it.

He flopped down under me, boneless, and I collapsed onto him, one hand still tucked under him, flat against his hip bone, sticky and damp with his come. He twisted his fingers and linked my other hand, resting on his wrist, with his. I could feel him breathing under me, his deep breaths lifting me, just a little.

I pulled out, slowly, and moved off him. I tied the condom and dropped it off the side of the bed, hoping I'd hit the trash can. One of our T-shirts was slung over the end of the bed, and I grabbed it, wiping us both clean enough, blotting up the wet spot on the sheets.

Beside me, Bellamy curled up, his limbs moving in, his back curving. I turned and ran a hand up his spine, and he shivered under my touch.

"Bellamy?"

"Yeah."

I rolled until I could prop myself up on an elbow and look down at him. He tilted his head over his shoulder to see me. His eyes were black smudges in the dark, his hair falling in thick strands across his face, blurring all his features. I pushed it back with my fingers, and he leaned into my hand.

His eyes closed. I could just make out the fall of his eyelids, the shadowy sweep of his lashes on his cheeks. "I like you inside me."

I dropped my forehead to his shoulder. I felt like he'd cut all the strings holding me up. "God, Bellamy. Me too."

He tucked himself up tighter, pushing me away, folding into himself. I pulled back again, one hand on his shoulder. He wasn't looking at me anymore. His face was pressed into the pillow.

"Sweetheart. You got to tell me what's wrong. I can't guess. Did I hurt you?"

He shook his head. His hair made slithering, inky lines over the white pillowcase. "No."

I dropped a kiss onto his shoulder. "Then what? Tell me, Bellamy. I don't care what it is."

His spine curved tighter, but it pushed his body into mine, aligned us. I lay down beside him and wrapped an arm around his waist, pulling us flush, easing his body against me.

"I like you here. With me," he whispered. I could barely hear his voice. It was a voice for dark rooms and intimacy and secrets. I brushed the hair from the back of his neck and pressed my mouth to the spot.

"Okay," I said, slow, trying not to let on how confused I was, but at the same time, wanting an answer.

"I'm afraid. That you'll regret this. I'm afraid . . . you won't understand."

I tightened my arm around him. "I won't regret it. And I'll understand. Maybe not all at once. But I will, Bellamy. Just like you understand about Eric and the band and how . . ." How lonely I felt. Bellamy got that, had always understood that. "I promise."

"You can't promise that." He sounded sleepy, like he had those nights on the tour bus, after he'd worn himself out at shows. He could have had anyone, those nights. Any night. Beautiful men and women, glittering, gorgeous, spectacular people who would have been happy to crawl into his bed. To give him whatever he wanted for as long as he wanted it. He'd never needed me. There'd always been other options, dozens of other options. And I was plain and boring and not exciting, broken and sad and lost. But he'd picked me. He hadn't picked anyone else.

"Trust me." I tried to lower my voice, to make it as soft as his, to make it a voice for confessions and sleep. "I know it's hard. But trust me when I say I'll hold on to this with everything I've got. I need you. I don't want to let go." I would do it, because he was Bellamy. Because I'd loved him from afar for so long. Because up close, in real life, he was even better than I'd imagined. He was real. And because I thought he'd do the same for me.

He rolled over, and I thought he'd argue more, or ask me something else, but he only looked up at me. I didn't think he could even see me in the dark. But maybe there was enough light after all, because he nodded.

I reached for him, and he came, pressing against me, throwing a leg over mine, resting his head on my shoulder. His arm went around my waist, and he pressed his palm over my hip, over the tattoo that symbolized everything he'd done with his life. Over the place where I had branded him onto my skin before I'd ever even known him.

He looked like he might say something else, but he didn't. He just held me to him, and we fell asleep like that, sated and tangled in each other.

I woke up in the middle of the night. I knew it was late, because after we'd dozed, we'd crept back downstairs and eaten dinner straight from Bellamy's fridge, and we'd talked, and kissed, and touched, and by the time we'd gone back to bed, it'd already been close to midnight. Not late by rock music standards, maybe, but late enough. And now the house was still around us, like it had itself been sleeping for hours.

I wasn't sure, at first, what had woken me. Then I realized Bellamy was awake beside me. He wasn't touching me or moving around, and I couldn't remember him making a noise. I just knew he was awake, from the sound of his breathing and the way he held himself in the bed. A little apart, a little too still, like he was trying not to be awake, or trying not to wake me.

I rolled toward him and laid a hand on his arm. "Bellamy? You okay?" I kept my voice a whisper, even though it didn't matter how loud I spoke. It felt right.

He nodded, but he didn't turn to me. I could just see the sheen of his eyes in the dark, staring up at the ceiling.

I scooted even closer, so I could feel my skin all along his, and rested my head on his shoulder. "Are you sure?"

The corner of his mouth curved up, and his gaze went from far away to right here, with me. He turned his head a little, just so he could see me. Our faces were so close I felt his chin bump my nose. "Yes, Micah," he said, a hint of teasing in his voice. "I'm okay. I'm just thinking."

"At . . ." I lifted myself on an elbow to see the clock on the other side of the bed. "Three in the morning?"

He shrugged, small, just enough to jostle me a little.

I swallowed, suddenly nervous. "Are you . . . *You're* not regretting this, are you?"

He shook his head right away. "No. I want it." His hand skimmed down my back, over my spine, soothing. "None of what happened before, when we argued, was what I wanted. I didn't want it to be like that between us."

"No. Me either."

Bellamy sighed. "Did you ever go to house parties when you were in high school?"

I shrugged. I was starting to get used to his weird changes in topic. I figured he usually had somewhere he was going with them. "Sure." Hadn't everyone gone? School had been okay for me—I hadn't hated it like Eric had, and I hadn't loved it. I hadn't exactly been popular, either, but boys who play instruments in rock bands get free passes on a lot of things. We'd gotten invited to parties, and we'd gone if there hadn't been anything more exciting happening.

"Did you like them?" He wrapped his arm tighter around me. "You always see these epic parties in movies, with all the furniture out on the lawn and bands putting on impromptu shows in the living room. They looked fun."

I thought about it. It seemed like a long time ago, even though it had only really been a handful of years. "They were okay. They weren't ever like that. Furniture on the lawn, yeah, sometimes, but a lot of trashed people puking on the same lawn. And we never played shows. Sometimes Eric brought his guitar. Mostly they were a good way to kill a Saturday night. But we . . . It was a small part of town. Maybe they're better somewhere else."

I glanced up at him, and he grinned at me. I knew how ridiculous it was, to try to keep a fantasy of those parties going for him. But I wanted to.

"I didn't go," he said, the smile fading a little. "I . . . I don't know if I wanted to, then. I think I knew they wouldn't be what I imagined. And I wasn't . . . I didn't have a lot of friends asking me to go, you know? There weren't a lot of opportunities. I told myself I didn't mind."

"Did you, though? Did you mind?"

He shrugged. "I don't know. Probably not really. But they're like . . . They're like this thing that you only get to do during a certain part of your life. You never get to go back and try again if you missed it the first time. You can go to a party now, but it won't be the same at all. That opportunity is . . ." He lifted his free hand, curled his fingers into his palm, flicked them out, like he was mimicking a firework. "It's gone."

"Like being a musician. A rock star," I added.

He nodded. "There shouldn't be an age limit on that. But there is, kind of. If you don't do it, start going for it, when you're young enough, you probably won't ever get the chance you need."

I ran my hand over his chest. I liked the way he tried not to shiver. "But you did that instead of going to parties."

"Yup."

I leaned up on an elbow, propping my chin on his chest so I could see him. "Bellamy. This is what you're thinking about at this hour?"

He smiled again, just a flash. He wrapped his other arm around me, holding me to him. "Do you regret all that time you spent trying to be in a band with Eric? All that effort? Now that you know you don't want it?"

I looked down, away. I knew he hadn't meant it to hurt. But there was no way to ask something like that without it being painful. He waited for me, didn't try to rush me, but he didn't try to take the question back, either, and I was grateful for that. Because now I was thinking about it. Maybe I'd been thinking about it for a long time. Maybe it was something, in the back of my mind, the back of my heart, that I'd been trying to come to terms with, since Eric had died. And now I wanted to get it out.

"No," I said finally. "That was who I was then. That was what I wanted. And even if it hadn't always been, I don't regret it anyway. It . . . made me. I'm who I am because of all that time." With the music. With Eric.

Bellamy nodded. "Good. I'm glad."

I met his eyes again. "You're not telling me you regret doing what you did, instead of going to parties, are you?"

He let out a short laugh. "Of course not. But parties weren't very important, in the grand scheme of things. Not for me."

"But . . ." I pushed.

"But I miss . . . I regret that there was an opportunity there and I didn't take it, and now I'll never . . . have that experience, whether it was good or bad, that so many other people have. I could have stood in the middle of it, and I didn't."

I pressed my lips together and thought about it. "That makes sense."

He pushed my hair back behind my ear, smoothing out the waves and tangles I'd gotten from rolling around in bed. "I feel like if I let you go, that it'll be the same. This once-in-a-lifetime chance that I have, and if I don't take it right now, it'll disappear." He stopped and took another breath, long, and let it out slowly. He wasn't smiling anymore. He was so serious. But he never looked away from my face. "I don't want you to disappear."

"I won't." My voice was a whisper, and I couldn't figure out how to make it come out any louder than that.

"Okay."

I thought about it, lying here with him in the dark, the warmth of him all around me. I didn't know what to say to make him believe me, what to say so that we could move past this. I knew it was important. I wanted to make it right, or as right as I could right now.

"You know that I feel the same, don't you?" I asked, softly. I wasn't sure if he was asleep, but then he shifted, tightening his arm, rolling toward me a little. "That I'm scared you'll finally remember that you're a rock star and I'm just me, and you could have anyone you want. Anyone at all."

"I want you," he said. Maybe my drowsy way of talking about this might work after all. "I'm not going anywhere, either, Micah. I don't want anyone but you."

It felt like he'd poured warmth into me, like he'd reached into all the deep, dark places inside me and set them alight. "That's how I feel. So we're even. Okay? Don't forget it."

He huffed out a tiny laugh. "Okay. I won't."

Bellamy was awake before me again in the morning. The space beside me was empty, the light was coming in through the thick curtains he had in his bedroom, and I didn't bother to check the clock. Just tugged my jeans on and wandered downstairs. I poked my head into the kitchen and living room, but he wasn't there. I went to the other end of the house. There was a set of double doors there, one open, and when I stuck my head in, I saw that the room was a studio.

It was so lovely that for a second I stopped and stared. It was bright, and it looked like every musician's dream ever, come to life. The floor was a butter-yellow wood, covered in colorful rugs. The walls were white, and they reflected the sun coming in through the high windows. That sunlight bounced off blue and green guitars, scattered in stands around the room, off the glossy white and black keys of keyboards, off the small soundboard tucked into a corner, off the slick black of coiled cords that spread out in every direction. At the back, I could see an open door, and through it, a drum set, a four piece, with cymbals packed so densely around it I wasn't sure how anyone could get through to sit behind it. The studio was grand, but comfortable. If I were still in a band, I would never have wanted to leave a room like this. I kind of didn't want to anyway. And Bellamy was sitting in the middle of it, on a worn white cotton couch. He had a guitar in his hands, and was playing it idly, his fingers moving over the strings like he was familiarizing himself with them again. There was sunlight on his hair, the yellow light running down his neck. I wanted to stare at him. I wanted to stop and remind myself that he was mine.

"Hey."

He looked up, flattening his palm, stopping the sounds the guitar made. "Hey."

I came and stood in front of him, hesitant, but he smiled at me, reached up to tug at the belt loop of my jeans. I sank down, sitting on the floor, so I could lean my head back against his hip.

"What are you playing?" I didn't care, really. I just liked listening to him pick out notes. I loved it when he played his songs. I loved it when he played covers. It was like learning songs all over again, songs I thought I knew well. But I didn't know them the way he heard them. I could listen to him, no matter what he did, all day.

He moved his hand, running his fingers through my hair, over the back of my neck, making me shiver. His hand rested on my shoulder, and I pressed mine against it.

"New stuff," he said, quietly.

"Yeah? I can go, if you want to keep working on them."

He tightened his fingers on me. "No. You could listen. I'd like that. Tell me if they're any good."

I laughed. "Of course they're good. I don't have any doubt of that." I turned so I could see him. "Do you?"

He shrugged. "I can't ever tell with my own stuff. If I think it sounds good, it doesn't mean much."

"But . . . all those songs of yours."

He smiled down at me. "Yeah. Those work, though. There's no reason that what I did to write those will work again. It's like a magic trick that should only work once but keeps working by accident. I keep waiting for it to run out."

"It's not like that at all. It's not magic." I remembered all the times I'd thought of what he and the band did on stage as some incredible magic, and wanted to kick myself. "It's talent."

He nodded. I didn't know if he believed me or not.

"That's it, isn't it? The anxiety. This is what it tells you. That you're not good enough."

His smile went even softer. "That's it."

"You should have someone with a better ear than me listen to your new stuff." I sat up a bit. "I'm not . . . I don't have any qualifications or anything."

"You're a musician," he said easily. "So there's that. And you're a fan. You were a fan before you knew me. Right? You like the music?"

I nodded.

"Your opinion counts, Micah. It'd matter even if you weren't a fan."

I smiled, my face tipped down so he couldn't see. "Okay, then."

"I've got to write for the new album, anyway."

"That makes you scared?" I asked.

His squeezed my shoulder, then pulled away. "I'm afraid that I'll do it wrong this time. Or that someone will realize I've been faking all along." He took a deep breath and shifted on the couch, the guitar making a tiny, gorgeous sound.

"You're not." I would be firm on this. "If you are, that means the things of yours I've taken for myself, your songs, your words, it means they're not real. And they are. They're important to me. They mean something. They're part of me. Don't take them away."

He shifted again. "I didn't—"

I sighed, steadying myself. Reminding myself that he couldn't tell himself to think differently. "I know." I turned around, rising up to kneel in front of him. I wanted to touch him, but I didn't. I just stared him in the eye. "I think . . . I think the fear, that worry that you're doing it wrong—it means you're on the right track. It means you're making something so important that it's scary. So big it can't be ignored."

He smiled, a small thing. "Maybe. It makes me happy too. Writing. Playing music. It always does. That's why I keep doing it, you know? I know I've been down, and all I've done is complain." I shook my head, but he kept talking. "But I do this because I love it."

I nodded. I knew that. I hadn't ever questioned it, or questioned that he was strong enough to keep doing it.

He did reach out to touch me then, brushing my bangs back, letting his fingertips linger on my skin, trail down my cheek and my jaw. "Micah. What are we doing?"

I shrugged. "What do you mean?"

"I mean . . ." His hand tightened on the neck of the guitar. "You're not going to be a roadie forever."

I shook my head, agreeing. "No. I won't. So what?"

"So . . . you won't always be with the band."

I shook my head again, slower, trying to figure out what he was getting at. "No . . . I wasn't really planning on it. Not that I don't like it," I added quickly. "Not that I don't like traveling with the band, and you." Oh. *Oh.*

A certain calm came over me. I didn't know what I wanted with my life any more than I had when I'd taken the job to be roadie to Escaping Indigo. I had no goals. No plan. It was frightening, beyond frightening. But, for a minute, I wasn't scared. There was a freedom in knowing that my options were open, that I could figure things out for myself. In knowing what I didn't want, and being okay with it. "I'm not going anywhere anytime soon, I don't think," I said. "And whatever happens, it doesn't mean I'll have to leave you. Even if I leave the band."

"What if you do, though?" I would never figure out how he did that, asked questions that should have been leading, all the while looking like he couldn't care less about the answer. Like it was mere curiosity that opened his mouth. "What if it doesn't work between us?"

I knew he did care, though. I knew he wanted the answer like I wanted to know all the tiny things about him. I sat back on my heels and stared at him for a second. His hair was falling a bit in his face, his bangs covering one eye, which had a smudge of eyeliner underneath it. His features were too sharp and his jaw was slightly too narrow to be conventionally attractive. He hadn't shaved yet, and he hadn't shaved yesterday, either, and the sexy scruff he usually had going was edging into a too-lazy look. But I still thought he was beautiful. I wanted him whenever I saw him. Or thought about him. Maybe it was because I was in love with him.

I took a breath. He held my eyes. I took the guitar from him, moved it to the floor next to me, careful with it. Then I leaned forward and put my head in his lap.

"My heart will break. If this doesn't work, that's what will happen," I said, trying for the same tone he'd used. I didn't think I quite got there, because I was telling the truth, and if I thought too hard about it, it ached. "And then I'll try to just be glad that I got to be with you for a while."

"Micah." His arms came up, wrapped around me, holding me as tight to him as he could. "You don't think that will happen, do you?" This time, his voice was breathy, no longer so unemotional.

"I don't know, Bellamy," I said honestly. "I hope not. I don't want that to happen." I closed my eyes, pressed my face against his hip. "I like being with you. No matter what. I want to be with you."

He ran a hand through my hair. It was too short to tangle his fingers in, but he twisted them against the nape of my neck anyway. "I don't think it will, either. I'll do my best for you, Micah. I will."

"I think that's probably all anybody wants." I thought about Eric, about everything he'd taken away from me by taking away himself. My goals, my hopes, my career. My whole life. And none of that compared to how much I missed him. How much I just wanted him back. And I hadn't been in love with him. I didn't know if I could do that again. I'd told Bellamy that my heart would break, and that was probably the truth. It was undoubtedly the truth. I'd said it like a fact, because it was. If it happened, though, I wasn't sure I could live through it. Go through all that again.

But I was willing to try. To give it my best. I knew Bellamy was scared too, and he was willing to give it a go. So I would too. I'd just believe that we could do this. That this wouldn't hurt me like I'd been hurt before. That I'd live through it again if it did.

He slid his hand down my back, running his palm over the bumps of my spine. "Stay with me," he said, quietly, into the stillness of the room.

I closed my eyes and let myself feel him all around me. There were apologies to be made, many of them, and there were things to work out, ways to figure out how we fit, how to be with each other. We had time now, though, and space. And for now, this was, like I'd told him, all I wanted. "Of course."

"So what we're going to do . . ." he pressed again, but he sounded almost playful or teasing this time.

"We're going to sort ourselves out," I said. "We're going to talk. We're going to be together. We're going to go back on tour for those last festivals and have fun."

"That sounds good."

I nodded against him. I thought it sounded pretty good too.

Explore more of the *Escaping Indigo* series:
riptidepublishing.com/titles/series/escaping-indigo

escaping indigo

BOOK TWO

skin
hunger

ELI LANG

Dear Reader,

Thank you for reading Eli Lang's *Escaping Indigo*!

We know your time is precious and you have many, many entertainment options, so it means a lot that you've chosen to spend your time reading. We really hope you enjoyed it.

We'd be honored if you'd consider posting a review—good or bad—on sites like **Amazon, Barnes & Noble, Kobo, Goodreads, Twitter, Facebook, Tumblr,** and your blog or website. We'd also be honored if you told your friends and family about this book. Word of mouth is a book's lifeblood!

For more information on upcoming releases, author interviews, blog tours, contests, giveaways, and more, please sign up for our weekly, spam-free newsletter and visit us around the web:

Newsletter: tinyurl.com/RiptideSignup
Twitter: twitter.com/RiptideBooks
Facebook: facebook.com/RiptidePublishing
Goodreads: tinyurl.com/RiptideOnGoodreads
Tumblr: riptidepublishing.tumblr.com

Thank you so much for Reading the Rainbow!

RiptidePublishing.com

acknowledgments

Many, many thanks to:

My parents, always, for all the things.

May Peterson and Sarah Lyons—your insights were invaluable and wonderful.

Alexis Hall, for reading an early draft of this and pointing out so many things that helped make this book something I actually liked.

Jim, for teaching me all the basics of drumming.

Ryan, for teaching me everything I know about music—not just how to be a drummer, but music theory, recording, the business of it, playing live, and everything in between—and for expanding my mind, constantly. I hope I've done you justice here.

Roan Parrish, for offering up an amazing list of potential band names when I asked for help—Escaping Indigo is gorgeous and perfect.

Avon Gale, for letting me introduce her awesome band Victoria Vincent to Escaping Indigo.

Last but very much not least, the Blanketeers, for everything you do—which is so much, and I am so incredibly grateful—and Cosy for being the absolute most amazing friends. All the love for you.

ABOUT
the author

Eli Lang is a writer and drummer. She's played in rock bands, worked on horse farms, and had jobs in libraries, where she spent most of her time reading every book she could get her hands on. She can fold a nearly perfect paper crane and knows how to tune a snare drum. She still buys stuffed animals because she feels bad if they're left alone in the store, believes cinnamon buns should always be eaten warm, can tell you more than you ever wanted to know about the tardigrade, and has a book collection that's reaching frightening proportions. She lives in Arizona with far too many pets.

Website: leftoversushi.com
Facebook: facebook.com/EliLangAuthor
Twitter: twitter.com/eli__lang
Goodreads: goodreads.com/eli_lang

Enjoy more stories like
Escaping Indigo
at RiptidePublishing.com!

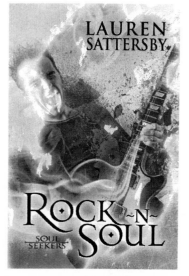
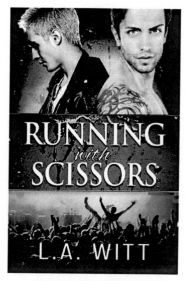
Earn Bonus Bucks!

Earn 1 Bonus Buck for each dollar you spend. Find out how at
RiptidePublishing.com/news/bonus-bucks.

Win Free Ebooks for a Year!

Pre-order coming soon titles directly through our site and you'll
receive one entry into a drawing for a chance to win free books for
a year! Get the details at RiptidePublishing.com/contests.

CPSIA information can be obtained
at www.ICGtesting.com
Printed in the USA
LVOW12s1832110717
540980LV00004B/683/P